I0730805

JOSHUA WHEELON
THE DEPARTURE
WORKBOOK PRESS
RECOMMENDED
LITERARY BOOK COMPETITION 2020

WORKBOOK PRESS LLC
187 E Warm Springs Rd,
Suite B285, Las Vegas, NV 89119, USA

Website: https://workbookpress.com/
Hotline: 1-888-818-4856
Email: admin@workbookpress.com

Ordering Information:
Quantity sales. Special discounts are available on quantity purchases by corporations, associations, and others.
For details, contact the publisher at the address above.

Library of Congress Control Number:
ISBN-13:   978-1-956876-18-5 (Paperback Version)
                978-1-956876-19-2 (Digital Version)

REV. DATE: 09/11/2021

DEDICATION

This novel is dedicated firstly to my mother, Gina Wheelon, who sadly did not get to see my work published. She was a great inspiration for me achieving my dreams and to do my best work.

Secondly, I dedicate this book to my grandfather, Hollice Wilcox, a man who inspired me to work hard at anything do and to be the best version of myself even with the temptation to give up and not do the work. If it weren't for him I would have given up years ago.

Thirdly to my dad, Burton Wheelon and siblings, Erin, Alyssa, and Stephen, who have always shown me love and kindness, even when I did not deserve it.

A final thanks to my Lord and Savior Jesus Christ who with His spirit, gives me the strength I need to continue on no matter what obstacles I face.

Dear Valued Readers,

I am honored and excited that you have chosen to embark on the journey of my first novel along with me. I do hope that you have a great time as I take you on this adventure through a futuristic world. A tale that involves religion, space battles, action sequences, a little bit of romance and so much more.

It is my hope that some scenes from the Holy Bible, which I have instilled within the novel, give you the curiosity to read for yourselves and embark on an even greater journey of self discovery. Even if you are not a Christian, there are many good principles that we can learn to live by. And every moment we spend studying God's word and spending time in prayer, we grow closer to Him. Being with Him brings me so much joy, and I want to share that joy with everyone.

Thank you again for embarking on this journey with me. I look forward to moving forward and taking you on this great adventure.

Sincerely,

Joshua Wheelon

PRELUDE

Near the Beginning of Time, Garden of Eden

Eve awoke in her husband's arms. He looked so peaceful as he slept. She reached up and stroked his curly, black hair. His hair was soft against the palm of her hand. She knew for sure that she loved him, and she thanked God every day for making her from one of Adam's ribs.

She stood up carefully, as to not waken him, and walked out of the thicket they had made into their home for the night. She looked around and admired all the beautiful plants and animals God had created and put in their care. As the wind blew through her long, red hair, she saw in the distance a brontosaurus as the enormous animal ate leaves from a tall tree. Zebras, antelope, giraffes, and bison grazed on the grass around the enormous dinosaur.

Up above, a flock of geese flew off in a V pattern.

Eve walked over to a nearby pond and jumped in for her morning bath. As she stood up in the water, she felt a heavy breath against her back. She turned to see a Tyrannosaurus rex. As the large beast stood by the shore, he lowered his mighty head to hers. She reached up and stroked his large muzzle. The giant beast gave a loud purring sound and then bent over, drank some water, and slowly moved on.

Eve finished her bath and came out of the water. She sat down on the ground and lay on her back in the soft grass to watch the water above called the sky.

As she lay there, she heard footsteps behind her and turned over to see the serpent as he walked out from behind a large bush. The serpent was three feet around with long front legs that raised his chest high off the ground. His back legs were six feet aft and held his body a bit lower to the ground. In total, his body was twenty feet long. His slimy skin was yellow with white markings.

The serpent made his way over to her. "Hello, Eve."

Eve sat up in shock. "How can you talk?"

"That isn't important. Tell me, Eve, what is your favorite fruit?"

Eve considered the question. There were so many to choose from, but eventually her mind came up with an answer she believed to be true. "I love peaches. They are so sweet and juicy."

"Indeed, but what about that fruit?" the snake motioned toward one tree to the left of Eve, "Have you tried this one?"

The tree was shorter than most trees but had longer branches. The tree's fruit was bright yellow and oval shaped. Eve instantly recognized the tree and gasped, "Oh, no! We can never eat from that tree."

"Why not?"

"Because God told us not to. That is his one rule. If we do, we will most surely die."

The creature laughed. "That is so silly, Eve. The fruit is not poisonous. Instead, if you eat of the fruit, you will be like a god. And you will know good and evil. Trust me."

Eve stood up and walked over to the tree. As she picked a fruit, she noticed that all the animals had stopped what they were doing and were looking at her in a strange manner. She opened her mouth and slowly took a bite.

The taste was so sweet in her mouth. Suddenly, someone grabbed her from behind and she turned to see Adam. He had an angry look on his face. "What have you done, woman? You know that God forbade us from eating that."

"But this tastes so good. Try it." She held the fruit up.

Adam took what remained in his hand and stared at the juicy remains.

He looked at Eve and then bit into the fruit.

"You are right! This is delicious."

Then Eve frowned as she realized something dreadful.

Adam frowned. "What is it, Eve?"

"We are naked."

Adam turned to see their reflection in the pond. "You are right."

They both felt so ashamed. Immediately, loud footprints could be heard getting closer and closer.

"We have to hide."

Adam grabbed Eve's hand, and they ran into the thicket.

A loud voice boomed, "Where are you, my children?"

Adam answered, "I heard you in the garden, and I was afraid because I was naked. So, I hid."

"Who told you that you were naked? Have you eaten from the tree that I commanded you not to eat from?"

Adam replied, "The woman you put here with me—she gave me some fruit from the tree, and I ate it."

Then the voice spoke to the woman. "What is this you have done?"

Eve answered, "The serpent deceived me, and I ate."

"Cursed are you serpent, above all livestock and all wild animals! You will crawl on your belly, and you will eat dust all the days of your life. And I will put enmity between you and the woman, and between your offspring and hers; he will crush your head, and you will strike his heel.

"Eve, I will make your pains in childbearing very severe; with painful labor you will give birth to children. Your desire will be for your husband,

and he will rule over you."

"Adam, you listened to your wife over my command. Cursed is the ground because of you; through painful toil you will eat food from the earth all the days of your life. The soil will produce thorns and thistles for you, and you will eat the plants of the field. By the sweat of your brow, you will eat your food until you return to the ground, since from the ground you were taken; for dust you are and to dust you will return. You will no longer live in Eden."

Suddenly, clothes made from leaves appeared on Adam and Eve. The sky turned dark and stormy, and lightning struck nearby. Adam grabbed Eve's hand, and they raced through the trees until they came to the edge of the garden. They stopped and looked over at the Tree of Life, which was much taller and grander than the forbidden tree. An object fell from heaven and landed on the ground in front of the tree. The object was a large sword, twice as big as Adam. The sword glowed brightly. Adam and Eve turned and ran out of the garden.

CHAPTER ONE

June 25th, Year 432 AE, Uncharted Region in Space

Captain Amet Bauer stood on the bridge of his vessel and stared out into the empty space that surrounded the ship. The stars were light-years away, and so was any civilization. He regretted taking this assignment every second of the day. Two years was a long time to be surrounded by the same faces. But the mission would pay well—one million databurts to split among a crew of five.

Eight months had passed since the *Del Rio* left the closest colony and five months since the last communication with civilization. Exploration vessels were much slower than most vessels, that would have taken only a few weeks, plus they had to stop and study many phenomena along the way. Their mission was to map as much of the far regions as they could and bring the data back to the Galactic Federation. They wanted to discover any inhabitable worlds that they could find before the Asiatic-Russian Alliance could claim them. Thankfully, Galactic Federation ships were better equipped for long-term missions.

"Captain Bauer." The cheerful voice of Mara Benson broke the silence from her scanning station.

"Yes, Surveillance Chief."

"I've detected a few planets about an hour from our location. One of them may be inhabitable."

"Set the course, pilot!"

"Yes, Captain."

James Colby, the redheaded pilot, began to alter the ship's course.

An Hour Later

After an hour of eager anticipation, the ship had reached the orbit of a magnificent planet—mostly blue, with some white clouds in the atmosphere.

"Magnificent." Amet began to smile. "Magnificent! Tell the rest of the crew! And James, get the bottle we were saving. After this, we can retire as kings!"

"Wait, Captain!" Mara chimed in urgently. "I'm detecting two ships approaching. They don't appear to be Asiatic or Russian."

"Do they appear hostile?"

"They are firing at each other. Wait, there is one more ship. Two of the ships are attacking one."

The German captain knew that with two factions in a newly discovered planet, his job was to promote peace. He had to act quickly so that both sides would view them favorably.

"Hail one of the attacking ships."

Mara did so, and on the video screen appeared a man with goldish-brown skin and a small mustache.

"הז הקולולנ איתמר אברהמס. מי אתה?"

"This is Captain Amet Bauer on behalf of the Galactic Federation. Do you speak English?"

"Yes. We learned English so that when you non-Jews return, we can tell you that you are not welcome here. This planet is ours." The man spoke harshly.

"I'm not sure what you mean by return. We've never been to this planet before."

The ship that was being attacked flew off.

"Are you kidding me?" The unnamed pilot shook his head. "You all came from this planet and left us religious folk here to fend for ourselves on a supposedly dying planet."

"You mean our ancestral home?" Bauer was ecstatic. "We've heard tales of such a place.

Some believed this place to be a myth. Most believers belonged to a cult devoted to a theistic view that one God created all this."

"That's what we believe. How many are in your cult?" The pilot was now curious.

"About one million, which is less than a hundredth of the population," Amet responded.

"That is sad. Hardly any of them will notice when the cult members are gone."

"Gone?" Amet was confused.

"This is a long discussion. Let us discuss more over dinner on the planet's surface. We will escort your ship down."

"Agreed." Amet nodded. "What can I call you?"

The pilot responded. "I am Benjamin Chaikin, lieutenant in the Israeli space force."

December 12th, 432 AE, Olympic City, on the Planet Washington

Chief Arliss Mars stood on the upper level of the east train station and looked down at the lower level. People were scurrying about. Some were on their way home and others on their way to work graveyard shifts. A few were out shopping. He noticed a bunch of people making their way out of the movie theater. The train systems were quite different from back on the ancestral home. Arliss had learned about the ancestral home in school.

The trains were the only form of vehicular transportation within the city limits, aside from ferries and small boats. Most people used them solely for transport. A train station, in fact, could be described as a shopping mall with no roof. A few fountains had been placed around the lower level for display purposes. Near the end was an escalator that led down to the dock, where two ferries waited to pick up passengers and take them across the Potomac Ocean.

A train stopped on the lowest of the five platforms, and people started to board. At the same time on the track above, a black security train that was much shorter sped through with red lights flashing and a loud siren blaring.

He saw many more people move out of the baseball stadium and join the already large crowd. At last, the time had come. From the farthest alley came several people all in white robes with crosses painted on their foreheads. Slowly they began to proclaim in unison.

"Praise be to Jehovah, Creator of all, and Father of peace. Salvation comes to those who seek. He welcomes all to his loving arms; our sins are washed clean, and he remembers them not. Join us, brothers and sisters, and you too may become pure."

Mars did not have anything against them personally, but he could not believe they would come day after day, even after the way the crowds acted. He reached up to his ear and pressed the comm.

"All right, brothers in arms, prepare yourselves just like every night."

He watched his men remain close, but not too close, to the group. People from the crowds gathered around from all sides and jeered at them. They yelled all sorts of insults. Suddenly, an enraged man emerged from the crowd.

"Give me back my daughter, you fools!" He pulled out a blaster.

Two guards hit him with stun blasts simultaneously. He fell to the ground, and the guards quickly grabbed him, pulling him toward a holding station. The mob got angry and started throwing objects at the guards.

"Brash it all." Mars shook his head and pressed the comm again. "Beta Force, move in!"

A siren sounded, and from multiple alleys, up to forty officers moved in, each armed with two stun blasters. Five of the guards made their way over to the group with the prisoner. Someone had hit a guard in the leg with an iron rod. One of the incoming guards stunned that man with a blast, but the crowd quickly covered him. After a few minutes, the crowd finally dissipated, and none were left, save for five of the group in white who were being monitored by the officers.

Mars rode the elevator down and shook his head all the way. As the clear door slid open, he made his way over to the injured officer who was being treated by a field doctor.

"You all right, son?" Arliss showed concern.

"I'll get past this, sir."

"I'd give him the week to recover and then have him reevaluated," the field doctor announced.

"Understood." Arliss nodded.

"Maybe I should not have fired my . . ."

"Stop right there, son." Arliss touched the young man's shoulder. "You did the right thing. He was armed, was he not?"

"Yes, sir."

"That's all that matters."

He turned to see Lieutenant Javers headed over.

"What is the deal, Javers? How did that guy get a gun?"

"His brother was a manufacturer and stole the blaster for him. Officers are on the way to pick him up and see if he stole any more. Guy says his daughter joined the Children of Jehovah. I just do not get them. Why do they persist in this nonsense when people are obviously not interested?"

"Takes a lot of courage; I'll give them that. I would give anything to let them speak through the Visual Message Boards from a secret location. But the prime minister banned that quickly against our, my advice."

"What should we do with them?"

"Did they hit anyone? Shoot anyone? Spit on anyone? Or yell profanities?"

"No, sir."

"Then we have to let them go."

"Yes, sir."

Mars could tell that Javers was irritated by his decision when he frowned and turned abruptly to head back to the five cult members. Javers hated them with a passion. Most people lost children to the group. Javers lost his wife. He watched as Javers released the five members and then turned to head back to the station.

One Hour Later in Uptown Olympic City

Mars rode the elevator up to the level his apartment was on. He thought about the situation that occurred that night. Things were getting worse, and something had to be done soon. Otherwise, chaos would ensue.

The door slid open, and he stepped off and walked down the hall to the end, waving his card next to the scanner by the door. The door opened, and he walked in. He put a smile on his face when he saw Angela as she stood by the window across the room and gazed out over the water.

"Hey, princess."

The seventeen-year-old girl turned and smiled at him.

"Father!"

She raced across the room, and he embraced her in his arms and kissed her on the head.

"Are you a sight for sore eyes, or what?"

He kissed her again, and they both sat on the couch.

"I saw you on the news. They said bad things about you. But I know they aren't true."

"Then I should be okay. You are always right."

He heard footsteps from down the hall and turned to see Marion come into sight. His beautiful wife smiled and motioned to Angela. "Off to bed, young lady."

"Yes, Mother."

She jumped off the couch and raced down the hall.

Arliss could tell something was wrong. Normally, his beautiful wife would scold Angela for running inside, but she looked tired. As she walked closer, he could tell she had been crying.

"What's wrong?" he asked.

She sat next to him on the couch. He kissed her on the cheek while she thought about what to say. "I do not know what to say to get through to that son of ours."

Arliss sighed. "What did Travis do now?"

"Nothing yet. He informed me that he has decided to join that wretched cult."

"What? Our son?"

"Yes. Aren't there any legal proceedings to keep him from joining them?"

she asked with hope in her eyes.

"No."

Arliss shook his head. The law was clear that anyone who chose to leave their parents for a religious organization could lawfully do so after they declare their intent to the authorities.

"Has he declared his intent?"

"Yes. A member is coming to pick him up in a few weeks."

"This is my fault. With the affair I had, I showed him I cannot be trusted as a guide in ethics."

"He claims that that had nothing to do with the decision, but he has not looked at you the same way since."

Arliss could see the look in her eyes. It was the same look she had after he confessed to her about the affair. While affairs in modern culture were popular, even praised, they had both agreed that they would not participate in such activities. But she had been spending a lot of time away from the city, taking care of her ill mother, and one night after a long day at work, he went to a bar while the kids were at a summer camp and met an old girlfriend, Cassandra Haydenbaum. They caught up on each other's lives and hooked up. He felt terrible about the incident and ended up confessing a week later.

"Go ahead," he told her. "Let me have it. I deserve this."

"I don't blame you for the affair. The thing is, I had the chance at an affair with an old flame of mine the same week, and I passed."

"Do you want to have one? Make things even?"

"No. I just can't comprehend why else our son would do this. I never thought much about the Children of Jehovah before. They seem peaceful. But why does everyone persist in hating them? Five of them were found dead in an alley last night. Then the incident happened tonight. I am so worried. How can they believe in something so strongly that even physical violence does not dissuade them? Who is this Jehovah that they follow so blindly?"

"I have no clue." Arliss kissed her on the forehead and stood up. "I'll talk to him."

He made his way through the living room and down the hall. He pressed a button, and the door on the right slid open. He saw his son on his knees by his bed with his hands on the top of his head, they covered most of his bright red hair.

Travis looked up at his father with a peaceful look. He stood up and sat on his bed. Arliss made his way into the bedroom and sat on the bed next to the pride and joy of his life.

"I gather Mother told you the news."

"Yes, she did. Can I ask why you decided to make this choice without consulting us?"

"I felt Jehovah speaking to me, Father. As soon as I asked him into my heart, I felt him inside, and I just knew this was the path he chose for me."

"Well, I will not stand in your way if that's what you genuinely want. You are allowed to change your mind. So, think this over in the next few weeks. If you still feel this way, I will take you there myself."

"Are you sure?"

Arliss nodded. "Yes."

"Okay."

"Now get some sleep, kid. You know I love you."

He kissed Travis on the forehead, got up, and made his way out of the room. As the door slid shut behind him, he found Marion waiting there.

"That wasn't much of an argument." She did not sound surprised.

"He's sixteen years old. All we can do is let him know we are here if he changes his mind."

"Okay."

Around the Same Time

Jack Priest stood on the balcony of his luxury suite. After he had heard about the Del Rio's discovery of the ancestral home, he had felt severely ill. The True God's lie would be exposed if this information were leaked. He had made several attempts to reach the Patriarch but failed so far. His right hand shook and threatened to spill the vodka from the glass he held. He wondered how the citizens would react. He would most certainly be booted from his position as prime minister of the Galactic Federation.

A loud beep came from inside the suite; he turned to rush inside and almost tripped on the edge of his white couch as he darted across the living room to his telecom screen. The green light at the bottom was blinking to indicate that a call was being received.

"Activate call." Jack stopped a couple feet from the screen.

The screen changed to the view of a large, burly man who sat on his couch with a bottle of whiskey and a huge bowl of cheese fondue with bread sticks dipped in it from the edges. He wore only a blue satin bathrobe.

"Priest. What is so urgent my friend?"

Jack struggled for a few seconds as he tried to remember the password. Then the right phrase came to mind. "The Penguin is loose."

The other man frowned and set his dinner on the glass table in front of him. "What's the issue?"

"The *Del Rio* has rediscovered Earth, alive and well. What are we going to do, Martin?"

"You told him to not say anything. Correct?"

"Yes."

"Great. We have a chance to keep this quiet. I'll call a meeting among the high brothers in a half an hour." He paused and leaned forward. "Can you pull yourself together in time, Jack?"

Jack could not speak.

"Jack?"

Jack shook out of his trance. "Yes. Of course."

"Are you sure?"

Jack confirmed. "I'll be fine."

"Okay. But take a sober serum, alright? I will, too. We all need to be at our best."

"You bet." Jack ended the call and went to the kitchen. He opened the cabinet next to the fridge and pulled out one of the electronic syringes with a light green fluid inside the chamber. He held the syringe up to his neck and injected the fluid into his body.

Jack opened the fridge. He knew that the sober serum, like most serums, should be digested with food. He saw half of the halibut he had at dinner, and he pulled that plate out. After he placed the dish of fish into the microwave, he turned the device on for a couple of minutes.

He paced back and forth until the bell rang, and he opened the machine and pulled the food out. He quickly scarfed the fish down. As he finished the last bite, the front door slid open and in walked his darling wife, Adalia. He had loved Adalia at first sight back at the college cafeteria twenty years ago. Thanks to medical advances, she did not look much older at all.

"Honey." The red headed beauty smiled at him as the door slid shut behind her. "I had such a great time at the opera. This one was particularly fascinating. Did you get your work issue taken care of?"

"Not quite yet. I have a conference call in about twenty minutes. It should not be too long, but you know how that can change."

"Well, remind them you have a beautiful woman waiting for you in your bed."

"I will." Making his way over to her, he embraced her as they kissed.

She noticed the syringe on the counter and the empty plate. "This is important. What is going on?"

"Nothing for you to worry about. Actually, this is confidential."

"Even from me?" she pouted sarcastically.

"Sadly, yes. Troubles of being prime minister."

Twenty Minutes Later

Jack sat in his office and faced the second telecom screen. Eight faces leered back at him from their own small screens, which filled his larger one. Their faces were obscured with black cloaks and hoods. Jack wore the same attire.

Finally, the figure in the top right corner broke the silence. "I told everyone we should not allow exploration that far out. 'Too risky,' said I, but did anyone listen? No."

Another chimed in. "This is not time for saying I told you so. We have too much at stake here. Who is on board this ship?"

Jack responded. "Captain Amet Bauer. He has no secrets we can use to discredit him."

"Then there is only one choice, my brothers." The second voice spoke again. "We have to eliminate them as quietly as possible."

"Are you sure there is no other option? Bribe them, perhaps?" The fourth figure was reluctant.

Jack shook his head. "They are military; they don't take bribes. I agree with the elimination, and I move to vote on this."

"Very well." The figure at the bottom, who sounded like the Patriarch, spoke up. "All in favor say 'aye.'"

All parties spoke at once. "Aye!"

"Done." The Patriarch stood up. "I will make the arrangements."

Jack replied. "I will let you know when they arrive."

The screen went blank, and Jack removed his hood and shook his head in disgust. How could he go back to his wife's bed after he had just voted for the execution of her brother? He got up, took off the robe, and placed the garment in the bottom drawer of his desk. Closing the drawer, he exited the office and made his way down the hall to his bedroom.

After thirty minutes of pleasure, he and Adalia lay next to each other in coherent silence.

Finally, Adalia broke the silence. "So, the fact that my brother discovered our ancestral home had nothing to do with the meeting?"

Jack's eyes widened in sheer terror. "He told you?"

"No." She shrugged. "I overheard the two of you. You seemed less than thrilled, though."

"Did you tell anyone else? Anyone at all?"

"No. I know better than that by now."

Jack released the air from his lungs with a sigh of relief.

"We have to keep this secret for now."

"Okay. I don't see why though."

"This will cause a mass hysteria since Earth was supposed to be dying. We have to be fully prepared for the fallout."

Inside, Jack was sweating. He knew that once Amet was killed, Ada would put two and two together. He had to speak to the Patriarch again, hopefully to come up with a peaceful solution.

CHAPTER TWO

0800, Next Morning, Hover Ferry Crossing to Another Part of Olympic City

"Kill her!" Jack was stunned as he sat beside the Patriarch on the bench. The two had agreed to meet on the ferry where they could discuss the problem without being overheard. "There has to be another way."

The Patriarch watched a gull fly overhead. "As long as she lives, she poses a risk. I know this hurts. The ship arrives in two days. She has to be gone before then." He rose and turned toward the stairs that led to the upper deck of the hover ferry and paused. "I'll give you until tomorrow morning. If not, someone else will—someone who doesn't care if he inflicts pain."

With that, the Patriarch started his slow climb up the stairwell. Jack stood up and walked over to the edge of the hover ferry. Shoulders hunched against the wind; he watched a pod of Orcas off in the distance. Ada always loved Orcas. They were one of the few Earth creatures brought with the people migrating from Earth. Her father was a marine biologist, and she spent so much time around them as a child. He decided right then and there that he could not let them kill her, nor could he kill her himself. He knew who he had to call. Picking up the mini telecom, he pressed the button for a contact. A tall man with graying hair and a few whiskers appeared on screen.

"Hello, Jack. Nice to hear from my twin brother."

"I need your help, James." Jack interrupted. "Ada is in danger and now that I'm warning her, I will be in danger, too."

"What about the minister's guard?" James suggested.

"I believe they've been infiltrated."

"That can't be. They have the toughest screening measures in the universe." James assured him.

"Not if the infiltrators had my help. We need to disappear for good."

James paused. "I know a way. It is risky but sounds like it is better than doing nothing. Get your wife and meet me at the balcony of your suite. I have a submarine that can get in undetected."

"Okay, James. See you then."

Jack turned off the mini-telecom and placed the device back in the holster on his belt. He turned and climbed up the stairs as the hover ferry landed. He made his way down the ramp and onto the dock.

0800, Elsewhere in Olympic City

Arliss walked down a long walkway from one upper train station to another as he patrolled the city that he swore to protect. This walkway was not too crowded. Neither was the water below. In the middle of the walkway was a balcony that stuck out and made a half circle. It was there he spied a man talking with a beautiful young girl who appeared to be about Angela's age. Judging by her clothes, she was obviously a prostitute, which was legalized forty-five years ago despite a formal protest from the Children of Jehovah. As he got near, he could hear that they were arguing.

The man spoke first. "You cannot leave this business, Grace. We need workers to stay for the long haul. If you got pregnant, we could fix that."

She answered. "I'm not pregnant, and I'm not ill. I have discovered Jehovah and found out who I truly am. This life is too filthy for a child of his. I have to strive for a better one."

"There is no better life for you. This stupid Jehovah of yours doesn't exist, and I won't let you go."

"Our contract is defined as 'At Will,' so you have no right to hold me." She turned to leave, but he grabbed both of her arms and shook her violently. "We'll see about that, you stupid girl."

"Is there a problem here?" Arliss stepped onto the balcony, and the man instantly released her and backed away.

"No, sir." The man shook his head. "We're just very passionate."

Arliss turned to the woman. "Ma'am?"

Though hesitant at first, the woman spoke up. "Yes. I believe he was going to throw me overboard or strangle me, like the other three prostitutes after they tried to leave."

Arliss remembered reading reports of the three dead women. He looked at the woman's arms and noticed marks where the man's nails had dug into her arms and left bruises. They looked identical to the marks of the other women.

"Well, Grace, is it? I can only do something if you press charges for the assault." Grace nodded and Arliss turned to the man. "Sir, you are under arrest for the assault."

The man scoffed. "Do you realize who I am? I am a personal friend of the prime minister. No official . . ."

"You have the right to remain silent. Anything you say can and will be used against you in a court of law." Arliss finished reading the man's rights and cuffed him. He touched his radio. "This is Chief Mars. I need an arresting unit to East Walkway A001 pronto."

A voice came on the radio. "Copy that, sir. May be an hour. There was a huge fight over on the far side of East Promenade C. We'll send someone as soon as we can."

"Negate that. I'll take him myself." He took his hand off the radio.

Arliss escorted the man to the nearest platform and onto the police rail car. He led the man into a holding cell and activated the force field as the man sat down. He wondered if the man had fibbed about being close to the Prime Minister. Thankfully, Jack Priest was also close to Arliss. They had attended the same prestigious school. Arliss had studied law enforcement, and Jack had studied political science.

The police lieutenant made his way over to the front of the rail car and sat as the door slid shut. The vehicle started automatically. No driver was needed because the rail system was controlled through a powerful network that ran the whole city. No fare officer was needed, either, because on police vehicles, a sensor detected a code in the officer's badge.

Arliss was thankful that the man had decided to use his right to be silent. The vehicle sped up to lightning speed through the emergency rail system until they reached the central station. Two police officers had waited to take custody of the prisoner. He followed all three of them onto the platform and down a small escalator to the police station. The large glass doors stood open, and all four of them entered the large building.

The station was spacious with the main room being three stories high. Arliss looked up at the other three levels that contained offices on one side and a gold railing on the other. All offices had glass walls and sliding doors. The prisoner was escorted to the front desk where a small circular object rose and scanned the man.

"Nathaniel Stonewell." A computerized voice spoke as the circular device created a holographic image of him. "President and CEO of Black Hearth Entertainment."

Arliss sighed. Stonewell was a big supporter of Priest in a financial manner. He also owned twenty strip clubs and prostitute rings on this planet alone. This man would most likely walk. Then what would happen to his victim, Grace?

"Would you like the presence of your attorney on record, Mr. Stonewell?" The computerized voice asked.

"I would." The man looked at Arliss and winked. "You are finished, officer."

"Chief Mars to you."

"Your attorney is on his way." The computerized voice interrupted.

"Thank you." Stonewell smiled, "Ah, yes. A close friend of Jack's, too. I wonder who will hold more sway. A former classmate or the man who is almost single-handedly holding his campaign for reelection together."

"I guess we'll see. Take him to holding to await his council."

The officers escorted the culprit through another glass sliding door and down the hall to a group of holding rooms. Arliss turned to see Grace walk in. "You could have waited until the morning."

"No need. I would also like to file a lawsuit against him for breaking multiple contracts that would have freed me sooner and for forcing me to work under threats of extermination of not just myself but my family."

A young man entered behind her. He wore the white robes worn by most Children of Jehovah.

"My name is Elias Faulkner, and I speak on her behalf." He held up a tablet. "This contains evidence of such actions."

1600 at an Unmarked Dock

James Priest stepped off his small sub and turned to the driver. "Go back under until I signal. We have three passengers coming with us. As soon as I signal, I want you to surface and then abandon the sub. You won't be needed after this."

The driver nodded and closed the hatch. James watched as the submarine submerged under the surface of the water. He turned and started to walk down an alley, but a man in a hoodie stood in his path. He tried to make his way past, but the man did not budge.

"Do you mind, sir?" James was irritated. "I'm in a hurry."

Then he heard footsteps from behind, and James tried to turn but was grabbed by two strong individuals. The first figure raised a foot-long blade and jabbed the weapon through the war veteran's heart. The unknown guys let him fall the ground and waited for him to die.

Once James had breathed his last breath, the three men went over to the river and the first one threw his blade into the water. One man dropped an underwater explosive into the water and moments later, a small explosion occurred. The men quickly turned and walked out of sight just as a jogger came along and rushed over to James' lifeless corpse.

1800 That Evening

Jack and Adelia sat peacefully on the couch and watched a TV show of a romantic nature on their large screen telecom. Jack glanced at the time. He knew that James would be there soon, and hopefully his daughter was on the way back home. Suddenly, the screen switched to a breaking news bulletin.

"Good evening, citizens." A beautiful blonde reporter sat behind a desk as she addressed the viewers. "I'm Alexandra Fitzgerald. A travesty has unfolded as a man was murdered close to the presidential suites. The reason has not been made public, but the victim is none other than James Priest, twin brother of Prime Minister Jack Priest."

Jack stood up with a start.

"Oh, dear." Adelia stood up and embraced him. "What on earth was he doing here? Was he joining us on this unexpected vacation you surprised me with?" Just as she finished her sentence, the door beeped, and she walked across the room. "Must be someone to deliver the news to us. They are usually better at their timing."

Jack finally broke from his shock. "No! Don't."

But the door had already slid open and a tall man with dark brown skin stood in the doorway in all-black attire.

"You don't look like security," she smiled nervously.

The man grabbed her and quickly stabbed a knife into her throat. He let her drop to the ground as blood spilled out onto the floor.

"Murderer!" Jack raced over, but the man dodged to the side and grabbed Jack from behind.

"You can't do this to me! I'm the prime minister!"

Jack felt instant pain as the knife penetrated his gut. And again, as the knife slit his throat. He collapsed to the floor on top of Adalia and breathed his last breath.

The man tossed the knife onto the ground and walked out. The door attempted to slide shut but could not because Jack's leg stuck out into the hall.

Around the Same Time on the First Floor

Paula walked into the presidential suites from the central promenade. She had really enjoyed her time with her best friend, Angela. Angela finally made her way in afterward.

"Did she say yes?"

Angela waited tensely and then smiled. "I finally got her to agree. After all, we are closer to school from your house. Did you tell your parents?"

"No. I think they are out for the weekend."

Both girls smiled. They raced over to the elevator, which slid open for them. They moved into the small box-like room and watched through the glass walls as they moved up level by level. When they reached the seventh floor and stepped off, a tall, brown-skinned man stepped past them. As he rode down the elevator, Angela looked back. She felt something was off about him.

"Race you to the door."

Paula ran down the hall. Paula was much faster; Angela was only halfway jogging. As Paula turned the corner, she slipped on a red substance and fell to the floor.

Angela stopped. She knew instantly what the substance was: blood.

Paula looked forward and saw her parents lying in an open doorway, dead. She screamed in horror and tried to run to them. Angela grabbed her and held her back.

"There's nothing you can do."

Thirty Minutes Later at the Hospital

Arliss raced through the sliding glass doors of the hospital. He stopped quickly to observe his surroundings. Several nurses rushed about from room to room. The waiting room was crowded with patients. One man, who appeared to be homeless, held an arm that was obviously broken. Arliss saw an info platform a few feet away. As he walked over, he brushed past one morbidly obese man in a hover chair and a young nurse who was trying to stop a patient from running out. He reached the platform and pressed the blue button on the panel next to the platform. A holographic image of a beautiful nurse appeared.

"How may I help you today, Chief Mars?"

"I'm searching for my oldest daughter."

"Angela Mars is right behind you, sir."

Arliss quickly turned to see Angela as she rushed over to him from the waiting room. He moved forward to meet her halfway and hugged her tightly. She hugged him even tighter in return.

"How are you, Princess?"

"Not well, but better than Paula." She let go and motioned toward her poor friend who sat on a chair in the far corner of the waiting room.

They made their way over to her. Angela sat next to her in the only chair left, and Arliss knelt on the other side.

"How are you feeling, Paula?"

"I think I broke my ankle when I slipped on the blood. The EMTs hauled me here."

"Do you know anyone who might have wanted to harm your father?"

She shook her head slowly, still in shock. "Everyone seemed to love him. Even that Jehovah cult seemed to at least not dislike him."

"What about your mother?"

"Not a chance. She was so charitable and gracious and kind. Who would do this?"

"Don't worry. I will do my best to find the ones who are responsible."

"The man!" Angela suddenly exclaimed.

"What man?" Arliss looked at his daughter.

"There was a strange man who was on that floor when we arrived. We got off the elevator, and he got on."

"Describe him."

"A couple inches taller than you, a bit thinner than you, dark brown skin, and he wore all black. I've been there several times, and I've never seen him nor anyone who dresses like him."

"Sounds like he's worth checking out." Arliss beamed with pride knowing that he trained his daughter well in the art of memory recall.

A voice came up on the loudspeaker. "Paula Priest to MR-A12."

"Here we go."

Arliss picked Paula up and carried her across to the medical room that had the tile A12 above the door. Arliss placed her on the bed as a man walked in with a light blue medical uniform on. The silver collar relayed his rank as a doctor.

"Hello all. I am Doctor Elliott Patterson. Are any of you family of the patient? We cannot treat her without parental consent."

Arliss pulled the doctor aside. "Her parents were murdered tonight."

"How unfortunate." He held up a tech pad and scanned some data. "According to family records, her only next of kin is James Priest, her uncle."

"Also murdered."

"I see. Well, we can transfer her to another guardian. Hopefully, one comes up soon."

Arliss noticed a pleading look from his daughter. He knew that Marion was fond of Paula, so she would not object, at least temporarily.

"I can claim guardianship. I am a friend of the family, and my daughter and she are best friends."

"Okay. I can diagnose her today, but until the forms are complete, I cannot treat her."

"How long will that take?"

"Five weeks."

"Five weeks! That is nuts! Is there any way you can speed that up?"

"As a chief doctor, I could skip the review and sign the form today."

"Okay, great." Arliss noticed the man seemed to be waiting for something and sighed. "How much?"

"Five hundred Databurts."

Arliss grimaced. He knew this would put the vacation he and Marion were planning off for at least a couple of years.

"Done."

He pulled his Data card out of his pocket and touched the glass screen to the tech pad. A small beep was heard, and he put the card back in his pocket.

"Okay." The doctor picked up a small scanning device from the medical tray and held the device over Paula's ankle. "Good news. The ankle is not broken. We will clean the wound, provide her with a set of clothes that we have available; the clothes she had on were soaked with blood. After a few injections of home antibiotics, she should be better in a few days."

CHAPTER THREE

20:05, The Same Evening

Arliss sat behind the desk in his office and waited for the telecom call to go through. As he waited, he noticed a bulky prisoner trying to make a run for the front door, but the door did not slide open. When he touched the door, a shock went through his body and the man fell to the ground unconscious. Arliss loved that security measure. The invisible field prevented any suspect currently under arrest from leaving the facility, but his officers and the general public could walk through with no trouble. This feature was also used to keep people with restraining orders out of the homes and workplaces of the people they were harassing. When those fields are triggered, security is immediately notified of the attempt.

Finally, a screen appeared, and he found his wife who was dressed in a simple white towel with wet hair. "Why do you insist on calling me when you know I've just taken a shower?"

"Sorry, honey." He couldn't help but chuckle, "I forgot. But I have a lot on my mind."

"Like what?"

"You haven't heard the news, then."

"What news?"

He informed her of the murders.

"That is so sad." Marion began to cry. "They were so nice. I don't understand who could do this and . . ." she gasped. "Oh, dear. Paula. How is she doing?"

"She and Angela discovered the bodies."

"Oh, that's right. Sleepover."

"Paula's okay, given what she's going through."

"Good. And Angela?"

"Doing okay. She gave us the description of a potential suspect. But there is something else. To get medical treatment for Paula's leg, I had to become her legal guardian."

"I understand," Marion agreed. "She is always welcome here. And she should be off to college soon anyway. Will they be coming tonight?"

"Yes, they are on the way now."

She gasped. "You should have led with that. I should slip into something more appropriate."

The screen went black.

"Goodbye to you, too, sweetheart," Arliss chuckled.

He leaned back in his chair and pondered the night's events. The big-wig he had arrested for assault of the young girl, the death of his good friend, and the adoption of Jack's daughter—now finally had some time to think.

The door to his office slid open, and a man entered, wearing a dark blue police uniform with a gray collar, symbolizing the technology department.

He knew the peace would not last.

Arliss sat up in his chair and dropped the peaceful smile from his face. "What is it now, Banks?"

"I got the footage from the hall before and after the murder. Permission to use the telecom?"

"Granted."

Banks turned on the telecom, and the screen appeared. A shot of the hall outside the prime minister's suite appeared. A door at the end of the hall slid open, but no one came through. Twenty seconds later, the door to the apartment opened, and Arliss could see Adalia Priest at the doorway. She appeared to be looking at someone. Suddenly she was yanked by seemingly nothing to where she faced away from the door. A knife appeared and shot up into her neck, like the knife had been jabbed. She fell to the ground, and Jack rushed into sight toward the empty space where the killer should be. They fought, but he fell backward, and the knife shot down into his heart, rose and, with one quick motion, sliced Jack's throat. The knife appeared to be tossed toward the middle of the room. The door almost slid shut but Jack put his leg out, and the door bounced off the leg and reopened.

Jack touched his wife's face and then breathed his last.

"Well, he obviously wore camouflage armor." Arliss slammed his fist against the table. "I thought that might be the case."

"The armor has a glitch in the second scene." Banks announced as the screen switched to a view of the elevator.

The elevator opened, and Angela stepped off with Paula. As they did, a man suddenly appeared out of thin air.

"Pause frame." Banks ordered and the frame froze.

"Gotcha!" Arliss jumped up with excitement.

"Should we put his face in the media?"

"No." Arliss shook his head. "Only show the photo to officers, security guards, and medical crews. We do not want to alert him. A killer that good will be extremely dangerous when cornered. This situation makes it legal to shoot on sight. Issue that with the order."

21:00, In a Different Part of the City

X made her way to the back alley behind one of the strip clubs and opened the door to a small storage room. The space was cramped with metal shelving on either side. Each level of the shelving held metal boxes. At the end of the room was another door, and next to the door was a desk with a mirror. She looked into the mirror and saw the reflection of a bald man with dark brown skin. X reached up and pulled the mask off, revealing a much smaller and bald female head with Caucasian skin. The assassin swung the mirror around to reveal a telecom and turned the device on.

An image of a young girl appeared.

"Is the task completed?"

"The kite has flown."

"That is great news, Mother. Father will be proud. Your next assignment is in the usual spot. This one is of equal importance."

"Understood. Sweet dreams, little one."

The screen went dark, and X swung the mirror back into place. As the cold-blooded killer looked into the mirror, she stripped down to nothing and pulled off all the remaining fake skin that covered the entire body. She stepped out of the leather boots, which had two inches of support.

She turned to one of the shelves and pushed the green button at the top. The front of the box slid up and she pulled out a foot-tall metal bucket and a bottle with a green chemical. Placing the clothes, fake skin and mask into the bucket, X reached down and picked up a hose. She flipped a switch on the wall and water fell from the hose. She waited until the bucket was half full and turned the water off.

After a brief pause, X dropped the hose and opened the bottle. She poured a little of the chemical into the bucket and the contents began to melt. Placing the resealed glass container back in the box, she picked up the bucket and poured the contents into a small hole next to the back door. Washing the bucket with water, X placed the metal cylinder back in the box and the door slid shut.

X stretched her muscles for a bit and then opened the next box down. She pulled out a small bikini made from various colored gems and a matching pair of pantyhose. After putting them on, the woman put on a pair of green earrings, a mid-length, straight blonde wig, and placed a couple sticks of bubble gum in her mouth.

She also put on a small brown coat and made her way back out to the alley. Once outside, X saw a tall man with an expensive suit and a flat cap. He held a long cigar between his lips and puffed smoke out at the same time. Based on his cheap glasses, she could tell he was disguised, too.

X put on an unbelievably cute smile and skipped over to him. "How would you like to party, sir?"

"How much do you charge?" He looked at her skeptically.

"Twelve Databurts. I dropped my price a couple for you."

"Not tonight. But here's a little something for your effort."

He pulled a Data card out of his pocket and handed the glass object to her.

"Thank you so much, sir "

She made her way back inside the room and over to her desk. Swinging the telecom around, she touched the Data card to the telecom and a picture of a red-haired man in military uniform appeared with a name to the right: Amet Bauer.

Southern Part of Washington, Desert Region

Ethan Darkmoon sat by the window of the hover train. As he looked out the window, he saw nothing but sand. Hover trains were awfully slow, and his trip would take hours. The bullet trains were faster, but they had more security. His uncles had told him to avoid security at all costs. The length of the journey was not important, only the outcome.

Ethan turned his eyes forward to the young boy who sat across from him. The boy had not said anything and had the same lonely stare. The young, dark-haired soldier wondered why the kid was so important to his grandfather. He could hear the old man's voice in his head.

"This boy is more special than anyone can comprehend."

Abraham Darkmoon's instructions were quite clear. The boy has no identity. Avoid security at all costs. Get the boy to New Seattle. Ethan's superiors would have a fit if they knew he was involved in anything illegal, although he was not sure how this was illegal. He glanced around at the few other passengers. One was an elderly woman who had been quite chatty at the station when Ethan helped her with her luggage. She was traveling to see her granddaughter, who was about to give birth to her first great-grandchild. Her other child was impotent from birth. She was fast asleep even during the occasional jolts when the train sped up and slowed down.

Another was a wealthy businessman, who seemed unhappy to be out in the middle of nowhere. He was even more agitated when a jolt caused him to spill a couple drops of red wine on his white suit. He began rambling to the waiter about the incident. Thankfully, he was on the other end, and Ethan could not hear him over the train's rumbling.

In the middle, across from the elderly woman, two young men laughed and hit on one of the waitresses, who seemed to love the attention. He knew their type. College students, probably getting their partying started a little early.

"You shouldn't judge people." The boy finally spoke, which startled Ethan. "Judging is for Jehovah alone."

"Then why do we have judges in court?"

"Those are for earthly matters. Someone's character is not."

"So, you believe this Jehovah?"

"I believe you are paying attention to the wrong people."

Ethan frowned as the boy looked past him. A tall man with a long, black coat stood in the doorway. He also wore a black mask with white markings and a black cowboy hat. Pushing his coat aside, he drew two large machine guns and fired at the two college students and the waitress. The two guys fell back in their seats as the bullets ripped through their flesh. The waitress stumbled for a second and fell onto their laps.

His next target was the wealthy man and a waitress who tried to bolt for the other door. They both were flooded with bullets that emptied the guns and fell one on top of the other. The elderly woman, who was now fully awake, screamed in terror but could not find the strength to move. The man tossed the guns aside, raced over, and grabbed her by the head. He twisted her head and broke her neck.

Turning back to Ethan, he then drew two medium length blades and rushed toward him. Ethan drew his firearm and fired a shot directly at the man's head. He half expected the stranger to keep charging, but the man fell backward onto the floor and lay there, motionless. Ethan stood up and grabbed the boy's hand.

"Come on." He turned to see two more men that looked exactly like the other as they walked down the next car. He led the boy out of that car as bullets whizzed past them. He found a side door and kicked the glass out. He picked the boy up in his arm and jumped out onto the sand.

After rolling a distance, Ethan stood up and turned toward the train. The two men stood by the broken door and watched him. They turned and walked out of sight.

Ethan picked up his backpack and opened the main compartment to pull out two silver blast rifles. He swung the black straps around both of his shoulders, and he let them hang at either side. He pulled out two blades like the ones the hitmen carried and attached their sheaths to his belt. Then he pulled grenade after grenade and hung them at his waist, too. The last two objects he pulled out were two water canteens. He tossed one to the boy and took a drink from the other. When both had their fill, he placed the canteens back into the large backpack and swung the supply bag around his shoulders.

"We have a day of travel ahead of us." He started to walk north, and then he noticed a piece of sand move toward them—a sand shark.

He ran toward the moving ground and grabbed the weapons at his side. He aimed them forward as the ugly beast leaped into the air. The creature was twenty feet long and thirty feet wide with a mouth big enough to fit twice around Ethan's head. Ethan fired two blasts right through the open mouth and slid under the body as an explosion of blood, flesh, and bone flew to either side.

06:00 *the Next Morning*

Ethan woke up inside the metal tent he had set up the night before. He looked up to see a different boy who was two years older. He sat up with a start and grabbed one of the blast rifles. The boy touched his arm gently.

"Fear not, Ethan. It's me."

Ethan looked into the boy's eyes and saw that he was the same boy. "Did I sleep that long?"

"No. As your grandfather told you, I am special. We need to get going. The time long prophesied is near."

"Prophesied?"

"From the old world. The ancestral home."

Ethan followed the boy out of the tent, and he capsized the tent to the size of a small box that could fit in his backpack.

"What is your name anyway? My grandfather forgot to mention that."

"I am one of the two that Jehovah has sent. You can call me Elijah."

Ethan remembered his grandfather telling of a character named Elijah from the biblical texts, the one who was stranded in the desert and the Lord, Jehovah, sent ravens to feed him bread.

"Named after the biblical character, huh?"

"No. That's me."

"Like reincarnated through the spirit?" Ethan was confused.

"And physically."

Ethan decided not to pursue further. His brain was beginning to get a headache.

New Hong Kong, on the Planet Japan, Asiatic-Russian Alliance

Esther made her way down the streets. This night was cold and bitter. She kept her eye out for the Night Watch. Anyone who got caught after curfew would be punished severely. She heard a noise behind her. Startled, the young woman turned to see a small cat run across the alley. Relieved, Esther turned and made her way over to the next street. She walked down the wide path to where a door was. She could breathe easier once inside. Esther was about to open the door when she heard another sound. She turned to see a twelve-year-old boy, who hid among some garbage bags. He was not of Asian descent.

"Shoo, boy." She knew that the Night Watch would think he came from her home and punish her because he was too young.

But the boy just sat there and looked up at her with peaceful eyes.

Esther's heart melted. She did not want another mouth to feed, but that was better than the alternative. She motioned for the boy to come in as she opened the door. The boy smiled as he got up and followed her inside.

"Who is this?" Esther's sister, Jasmine, spoke from her normal spot by the window as she sat in her hover chair.

Jasmine had been wheelchair bound after an accident in the mines where she worked as a nurse for the injured miners. Now Esther worked double shifts at her factory to keep the same amount of Yen coming in, if not more.

"I found him by our door."

"Interesting. What is your name, boy?"

"I am one of the two, but you can call me Moses." He spoke clear English without a Russian accent.

"Well, Moses. I would like to read your fortune."

"Oh, please don't scare him off, sister." Esther scolded her.

"Oh, nonsense. He seems brave to me."

Moses sat next to her at the table, and she took his hands, closed her eyes, and began to hum. As Jasmine hummed, she quickly stopped and opened her eyes. Her eyes widened in terror. "I see so many horrible things, but somehow you survive for a time. Then a violent death."

"Jasmine!" Esther scolded her again.

"I really see that." Jasmine released his hands and shrugged.

"I don't care. He's a child."

"Don't worry." Moses looked up at Esther. "Her vision came from Jehovah. I need to get to a transport as soon as possible. The time prophesied is near, and there are those who believe they can prevent this."

"Are you from that cult? They were all slaughtered by the Night Guard. You poor thing." Jasmine hugged him.

"If you must, I know a guy." Esther walked over to her telecom. The screen was locked by order of the Night Guard past 8 p.m. and before 8 a.m.

Esther pulled a small black circular device out of her purse and placed the object under the telecom. A small green light appeared on the object, and the telecom turned on. Shortly afterward, the screen showed a man with a bald head and black mustache.

"I told you never to call me here, my love."

"But Tao, this is important."

Esther explained to him what the boy had told her.

"Very well. I have a night pass since the cargo I am hauling is on behalf of the Asian High lord. I will stop by on my way to the space dock."

"Thank you, Tao."

Jasmine blew him a kiss and then took the special device off the wall. The telecom turned off.

"How come you never told me you had one of those?"

"Because you don't know how to be careful, big sister." Esther put the object back in her purse and went over to the kitchen. "Who's hungry?"

CHAPTER FOUR
Babylon, 539 BC

The desert heat could be felt as the young Daniel walked along a street in Babylon. He wiped the sweat off his brow with the sleeve of his tunic and continued. He saw a merchant who had a cart full of dates. He tossed a couple of coins to the merchant and grabbed a few dates from the top of the pile. As he ate the dates, he turned down a smaller street and walked up a bunch of steps to his apartment. Making his way inside, he finished the dates and walked over to a window that overlooked the main street.

He knew that he could get punished severely for what he was about to do. But his action was justified. Praying to Jehovah instead of King Darius was made illegal. But Daniel could not rightly pray to a man over his God. He bent down by the window like he had every morning, rested his elbows on the windowsill, closed his hands, and bowed his head.

"Father in Heaven! How great you are! You watch over me day and night. I thank you for the many blessings you have provided. You truly are . . ."

His prayer was interrupted as the door to his home was kicked in and four men entered.

"What is the meaning of this?"

One of the men was short with dark hair and a thick beard. "You know praying to anyone other than your king is illegal."

"I only pray to my God who said I shall worship no one above him."

"Take him," the man commanded. "The law will judge this scoundrel."

The Following Afternoon

Daniel stood at the edge of a door that led to certain death. His arms were shackled and chained, and two guards stood beside him with spears pointed at his head. He heard the growls of the hungry beasts from the darkness that laid before him. The man from earlier stood nearby. "I am finally going to be rid of you, Jewish scum. Will your God save you now?"

"If that is his will." Daniel smiled.

"Push him in."

"Wait!" They heard shouting and turned to see King Darius run from the palace and over to them in a frantic hurry. He stopped and took a moment to catch his breath.

"You can't do this; I will not allow you to harm my good friend."

The man interjected, "Your Majesty, according to the law of Medes, not even you can change this law. We have to keep the law, or we become a lawless people."

The king looked at Daniel with tears in his eyes. "I wish I could change this law." He hugged Daniel. "May the God you serve protect you."

The guards prodded Daniel into the dark tunnel and closed the door behind him. Daniel slowly made his way through the tunnel and into the middle of a dark room. The lions were resting along the walls, but one looked up and saw him. The hungry beast stood up and roared loudly. The others joined in and formed a circle around Daniel.

The first of the large cats moved close to Daniel and roared viciously, but a great light appeared, and a tall man with large wings appeared within the light. The newcomer raised his hands.

"Close your mouths, you unclean beasts. This man is under God's protection."

All the lions laid back down and went to sleep.

The man disappeared.

Daniel found a large stone and sat down.

Early the Next Morning

The next morning Daniel woke. The grown lions were still asleep, and two cubs were playing nearby. He heard the door open.

"Daniel!" The voice of Darius echoed through the room, "If you are still alive, please come out. I pardon you."

Daniel stood and walked out of the room and down to the door where the overjoyed king hugged him and escorted him out.

Daniel's accuser came out of the palace and looked at Daniel with shock on his face.

Darius commanded in a loud voice, "Guards, for this man's trickery throw him and his three companions into the lions den."

"Oh, please no."

The man fell to his knees and begged. But two guards came forward and grabbed him. They threw him and the three that were with him into the lion's den. The door shut, and the four men pounded on the door. They turned to see two of the lions rush towards them.

Back to the Present, January, 433 AE

Arliss sat in his home office and contemplated everything that had happened in the past few days. He wondered how long the drama would continue. He noticed Travis' bedroom door open, and Travis walked out. He sat down on the couch next to him.

Travis broke the silence. "So, I have a new sister now."

"Yes." Arliss suddenly found himself laughing hard.

Travis joined in. They laughed for quite a while. Finally, they managed to stop. But the laughter had been an incredibly good release, Arliss felt.

"So, you still want to join the Children of Jehovah?"

"Yes, Father." Travis confirmed the fears running through Arliss' head. "They know the true way to live, the way long forgotten by most of our kind. That marriage was for one man and one woman. If we all chose to live that way, there would be no violence and suffering."

"That would be nice, I guess. Of course, then I'd be out of a job."

"Didn't you have other aspirations growing up?"

"I planned on being a politician, like my father." Arliss nodded.

"What happened?"

"Your grandparents were murdered. From then on, I wanted to be on the security force to find the crooks that commit such violent crimes and put them away. I switched my major, and the rest was history."

"What if you hadn't pursued that? Perhaps you would be prime minister."

"Perhaps. Not sure that is the best occupation right now. Also, I would not have met your mother. She was studying law enforcement in the legal sense. She is the best prosecuting attorney we have. But if I had not switched, you would not have been born. Speaking of your mother, she should have been home by now."

Just then the telecom flashed on instantly, and a doctor appeared.

"Officer Mars?"

"Yes."

Arliss and Travis both stood up.

"I'm Dr. Wesley. I'm calling to notify you that your wife has been admitted to the hospital."

"What for?" Arliss' heart began to race.

"She had a massive stroke during a court trial today. She is in our intensive care unit. I would hurry."

Travis almost fell backward, but Arliss grabbed him as they both let tears come. "We need to be strong for your sisters. Wait here while I get them. We'll go together."

Arliss raced to Angela and Paula's room, and the door slid open. Both girls sat on the bed with school pads in front of them.

"What's wrong, Father?" Angela stood up quickly.

"Your mother had a stroke at work today. She's in the hospital."

"Oh, dear."

Angela and Paula made their way to the doorway and hugged him. "What about Travis?"

"He's waiting in the living room. We should go,"

They followed him down the hall just as the front door slid shut. Travis was no longer in the room. "I guess he couldn't wait. Let us go and meet up with him there."

Thirty Minutes Later

At the hospital, Arliss, Angela, and Paula sat in the small room near the bed. Marion looked so peaceful as she lay there with the thin, brain stabilizer circling her head. The doctor had told them that she would not last the night, and hospital policy demanded that she be removed from stasis soon because she was a donor. But Arliss demanded to wait for his son. He wondered where Travis went and how they beat him there.

The doctor came in again. "I'm sorry, but I cannot wait any longer. The policy is clear on these matters."

"Just a few more minutes!" Arliss felt his hand as he reached for his blaster as he stood up. "Her son will be here soon."

"Should I get security?" The doctor cautioned.

Finally, the door slid open, and Travis walked in. He was followed by a short, balding man in a white robe.

"Oh, can someone get this nut out of here?" The doctor seemed appalled.

"Father, this is Reverend Timothy Franton, my teacher. I would like him to pray for Mother."

Arliss took his hand away from the blaster and placed it on Travis' shoulder. "I'm sorry, son. There is no hope. She is gone."

"There is always hope with Jehovah." Travis replied.

"This is ridiculous!" The doctor started to move toward the bed.

Arliss found himself reaching for his blaster again. "Just let him do this. Give my son peace of mind."

"Okay." The doctor threw up his hands and backed up. "But do hurry. I have a busy schedule."

Arliss could not believe that he found a doctor he disliked more than the previous one.

Reverend Franton walked to the bed and placed one hand on Marion's forehead and his other hand on her chest.

"Jehovah, our Father in Heaven, this woman needs you right now. If it be your will, Lord, heal her and do not take her from her loving family. Whatever comes, give them peace, in your Holy Name, Amen."

Timothy stepped back, and Arliss took his hand away from his blaster and nodded to the doctor.

The doctor moved in and took off the brain stabilizer. Then Marion opened her eyes and gasped for breath. The doctor almost fell backward with disbelief. Arliss rushed over to her and sat beside her.

She spoke weakly, "What's going on?"

"What's the last thing you remember?" Arliss asked her, as he could hardly believe that she was alive, let alone awake and talking.

"I was in the courtroom, and then I started to feel numb. I was muttering nonsense, then I saw darkness and woke up here."

"The doctor said you were brain dead. He just took you off life support, and then you woke up."

"How? How am I still here?"

"Jehovah answered our prayer, Mother." Travis replied.

Angela jumped up and hugged her mother.

"Okay. Let us give her some space." Arliss stood up. "She needs rest, I'm sure."

He looked at the stunned doctor who could barely manage a nod. After Travis and Paula gave her a hug and a kiss, they all left the room.

"I can't believe this." Paula turned to Travis. "Can you tell me more about this Jehovah?"

"Sure." Travis walked down the hall with her and Reverend Franton.

Arliss sat down in the waiting room, and Angela joined him.

"What do you make of this, Father?" She was curious.

"I have no idea." He shook his head. "That should be impossible. But I have seen some strange things happen before. I just always thought the people they healed were faking being sick or blind.

Angela added. "Could this Jehovah they talk about be real? This cannot be pure chance. That doctor certainly would not help them fake something."

Arliss shook his head. "I don't know, Princess. All I know for sure is that I'm glad we still have your mother with us."

January, 433 AE, 19:00, Olympic City, Docking Port

Amet Bauer sat at the counter of a bar near the docking port. He stared at the half-empty glass of beer that sat in front of him. He was glad to be back home. And he was glad that his ship had done more than he had ever dreamed of. Rather than discovering a new planet, they had found the ancestral home of the human race. He wondered why news of the discovery had not been released yet and why he had been told by General Branson to keep the news quiet. He had a sick feeling in his stomach that something was not right.

The half-drunk explorer noticed a security officer walk in and make his way to the counter near him. The man was around 6 feet, 2 inches, a tad shorter than Amet, had short black hair, and good smile.

"Glass of wheat beer." The man told the bartender who poured his drink.

Amet was about to invite the man to join him when he felt someone touch his shoulder. He turned to see a pretty, young prostitute. She smiled at him and played a little with her curly blonde hair.

"How about you come up to my room, sir? You look like you are celebrating something. Promotion perhaps?"

"No thanks, doll. I have a wife. Call me old-fashioned, but I won't be with anyone else."

"That's sweet. Well, let me know if you change your mind." She set her card on the counter and at the same time jabbed a blaster into his waist. "Let us take this to the back. No sense in scaring off the fine customers."

He shot a look toward the security officer who seemed to be too busy talking to the heavy-set bartender.

Amet stood up and walked toward the door with the young gal close behind. But as he passed the security officer, the man turned and quickly knocked her blaster to the floor and had his pointed at her.

"You're under arrest, miss," he stated.

She quickly kicked the gun out of his hand, dropped a smoke bomb and ran out the back.

He coughed for a moment and then rushed after her. He made his way out the back and came back in after finding no one. He made his way over to the stunned Amet.

"I can take your statement here if you like, sir."

"I'd rather do so at the station. I have a feeling she was trying to kill me, Officer-"

"Mars. Arliss Mars."

Twenty Minutes Later, Security Station

Arliss and Amet sat in one of the holding rooms at the station. "So, you discovered the ancestral home, but the government wants you to keep quiet about it?"

"Makes no sense, does it? Until I thought about it on the way here."

"Yes." Arliss was intrigued.

"The reason we left our ancestral home is because the planet was dying, according to most scientists. But somehow all data pertaining to the location was lost. This is proof that the scientists were either wrong or lied in order to get everyone who was not religious off the planet and separate the God-believers from us. Then no one would contradict their theories of evolution and the Big Bang. Which reason do you think they would kill for?"

"My instincts say the second one." Arliss admitted.

An officer came into the room. "Sir, the man who claimed to know the prime minister wants to speak with you. He and his attorney. The witness has disappeared. We have no evidence other than your word."

Arliss cringed. "Release him. We have too much on our plates with Priest's assassination."

"Yes, sir." The officer left.

Amet was taken aback. "Assassination?"

"Yes. Yesterday. You didn't hear?"

"I arrived an hour before we met. The general did not tell me this. Do you think they are connected?"

Arliss thought for a second. "I find it highly improbable that they aren't. But if I bring this to most officials, they may be . . ."

"Yes?"

"The new prime minister, Alex Harper, was also classmate of mine in school before I switched majors. I do not think he would be involved. I will set up a safe house for you with only officers I trust. Then I will go see him. He might know what to do."

CHAPTER FIVE

Forty Minutes Later in the Ministry Office Building

Arliss sat in the waiting room at the government headquarters. The newly appointed prime minister was in a meeting and should be available soon. The building was rather empty for a workday, and he wondered why. He then remembered that this was a Saturday. So many things had gone on this past week that he had forgotten to track the days.

He stared out at the bay and watched a pack of gollins making their way toward deep water. Gollins were similar to dolphins on earth but twice the size, and they have been known to attack humans that get too close. A bit closer in, he noticed two hover boats racing toward a buoy. Shortly after, a security submarine arose from the water and followed the daredevils with a flashing red light. Racing in public waters was illegal because there was too much danger.

His thoughts were interrupted by the secretary. "Sir, the prime minister will see you now."

Arliss turned to see the receptionist as she stood by the open doorway.

"Thank you, miss."

Arliss walked inside and saw Alex, who stood by his desk with reading visors over his eyes and a digital pad in his hand. He looked up to see Arliss and placed the pad down. He took off the reading visors and walked forward.

"Arliss Mars, as I live and breathe," Alex's voice boomed across the room.

Arliss held his hand out, but Alex hugged him instead.

"It's been a while, hasn't it, Alex?" Arliss smiled.

"Yes, it has. Can you believe it? Me as prime minister. I wish it were under better circumstances. How is Paula holding up? I heard you and Marion adopted her."

"She's doing okay. Upset, understandably, but she's adjusting to her new home really well."

"That's good. No one should have to lose their parents that way. But I'm guessing you are here on official business."

"Yes. Also, to congratulate you, of course."

Alex sat down behind his desk and leaned back in his chair. "So, what can I do for you?"

Arliss explained the situation with Amet in great detail.

"I don't know how I haven't heard about the discovery before. So, you think this may have something to do with Priest's assassination?"

"I wouldn't be surprised if it did. I think we need to get this information out ASAP. Then they will not be able to keep this under wraps. I have placed the ship's captain and his crew in protective custody. He gave me an info drive with proof of the discovery—images of the planet and images of Earth that are identical in every way."

"Perfect." Alex turned on the telecom screen on the wall and a middle-aged woman appeared. "Secretary of Media Davis, let me introduce you to my good friend and Chief of Civilian Security, Arliss Mars."

"Good afternoon, gentleman. How can I help you?"

Alex responded. "Actually, I would prefer you join us in my office. This matter is too critical to say over a telecom."

"Of course. Give me a couple of minutes."

"See you then." Alex turned off the telecom. "Actually, I was meaning to look you up, Arliss. The chief of ministry security has severely fallen down on the job. Failing to update systems would have made it impossible for that assassin to get in. Are you up for the job?"

"Me?" Arliss was stunned. "I'm flattered, but I'm sure there are more qualified candidates."

"Who I cannot trust as far as I can throw them. Come on, Arliss. It is triple the pay you make now, and you get a government suite. Much more room than what you have now, I am sure. Plus, guards watching out for your family 24/7."

"Well, when you put it like that, I accept."

"Great. Let us toast on it. He opened a cabinet that was behind his desk and pulled out two glasses plus a bottle of whiskey and poured a shot into each. He handed one cup to Arliss, and they clanged their glasses together. They both gulped down the shots and set the glasses on the desk.

The door slid open, and Davis entered. She waited for the door to slide shut and then spoke up, "So what is the critical matter, sir?"

"Well, two matters actually. First, I am replacing our chief of ministry security with Arliss Mars. His failing to protect the last prime minister should be reason enough."

"I didn't see that one coming," she joked.

"Also, an exploration ship has discovered our ancestral home, Earth."

Her eyes lit up. "Truly?"

"Yes. Arliss here has an info drive with all the information."

Arliss pulled the small device out of his pocket and handed it to her.

"Now, Martha, we need to get this out ASAP. We believe there is a group trying to keep this secret because the scientists lied to the entire world's population so that they could separate us from the God-believers and create their own government. We believe this is the reason for Priest's assassination. He must have been trying to get this information out."

"Good heavens." Martha shook her head. "Jack was a good friend of mine."

"I know," Alex held her hand. "But we can't let his sacrifice go in vain. Tell no one the reason for the press conference. We need this ready ASAP. We only mention the discovery for now and the change in security chief. Find reporters off the street if you must. I'll be ready in twenty-five minutes."

Twenty-Five Minutes Later

Alex and Arliss stood in the back room near the entrance to the stage. Arliss barely had time to call Marion and tell her and arrange a security transport for his whole family to the ministry suites, an area Paula was already used to. He also had changed to the new uniform, most of which was dark blue but the light blue on shoulders, chest area, and upper arms was outlined in gold, and this uniform had a turtleneck, which was also gold.

Martha stood at the podium while a bunch of reporters stood on the floor below with microphones and digital pads. "Thank you all for coming to this at short notice. I give to you Prime Minister Alex Harper."

Alex walked out and shook Martha's hand before she joined the security officers in the back. He turned toward the crowd and waited for them to quiet down. Then he raised his right hand.

"Thank you all. Your support during these times is much appreciated. We are facing some tragic events today with the assassination of Prime Minister Jack Priest. He and his wife will be missed. But as a nation, we must move forward. In order to do that, changes must be made. Due to the failings in the ministry security, I am relieving Chief of Ministry Security David Waterworth immediately. In fact, I would like to introduce you all to his replacement. The new Chief of Ministry Security, former Chief of Civilian Security, Arliss Mars." Arliss walked out, shook hands with Alex and took his place next to Martha. "This is not the only announcement I have to make. Recently, an exploration vessel known as the *Bombardier* has discovered the location of our ancestral home, Earth." Alex paused while the reporters began to ramble with each other excitedly. "And Earth is completely intact, which means our founding fathers were wrong about the planet dying. There is, in fact, a civilization there made up of Christian believers who believe in Jehovah the God that is currently being worshiped by the Children of Jehovah. It is also inhabited by Muslims who believe in a similar God named Allah. They are currently warring with each other. I plan on traveling to this planet to negotiate a treaty that will benefit both sides equally and to put protection for them from the Asiatic-Russian Alliance. I will also bring a team of delegates with me to start an embassy on Earth. I will now open up for questions."

"When can we reclaim Earth as ours?" asked one reporter.

"The question was when can we reclaim Earth as ours. I have no plans to do so. We did choose to leave the planet, so it is no longer ours. We were given false pretenses but not from the people inhabiting that planet. The nations of Israel and Islam have more claim to the planet than any of us do. Once they become a part of the Galactic Federation, if they choose to do so, then if certain people want to move back, the process will be the same for moving to any planet within the Galactic Federation. Not all requests will be granted as there are far too many people to let everyone go there."

Around the Same Time on the Planet China

General Zhang stood in his office and watched the telecom broadcast of Prime Minister Harper that his spies had managed to pick up. He turned it off as the door slid open and an officer rushed in with black armor and a black helmet. He carried a laser sword at his side.

"You asked to see me, General?"

"Commander Ong. You've no doubt seen the teleconference our spies have intercepted."

"Yes, General."

"Prepare our best fleet. We are going to take Earth for ourselves and wipe those God-believers out of existence. Then we will see what resources we can mine from there. Hopefully, oil and gold."

"Yes, General."

As Commander Ong turned and raced out of the room, the war-torn general sat behind his desk and pulled out a cigar from his drawer and lit it. He did not care much of Earth's significance. He cared only that losing Earth would appear to be a serious blow to the Galactic Federation.

January 4, 433 AE, 08:30, Docking Port, Olympic City

Ethan walked down the hall of the Ministry's High ship. The young man next to him was Elijah, somehow fully grown in a matter of days. They were both disguised as cooks. The guards were obviously still following the procedures of the old chief because the new chief, Arliss Mars, had walked in and scolded them after the strange pair had already gotten through security.

As they made their way into the mess hall to report for duty, Chief Mars walked past and briefly made eye contact with them. Ethan felt extremely relieved that the new chief did not suspect anything. They entered the mess hall and were ordered to go into the kitchen and start peeling potatoes for the dinner in a couple of hours. Ethan was fortunate enough to have learned how to cook from his grandmother, and Elijah seemed to follow his lead rather well.

As the ship took off, the large pot of boiling water they were placing the peeled potatoes in almost tipped, but Ethan and another cook who was Hispanic caught the pot before it could tip fully over.

"That would have been a disaster." The other cook smiled. "You two are new, aren't you? I'm Horacio."

"Ethan, and this is Elijah. Yes, we are new."

"Not to worry. I am the chief chef. I see a lot of potential with you specifically. If you are having questions, don't hesitate to ask."

"How long will this trip be?" Elijah asked.

"A few weeks to get to Earth, a month or so there, and a few weeks back. So about three months."

"Sounds like an adventure." Ethan exclaimed. "Will we get to see Earth?"

"Doubtful. We do not normally get granted shore leave. Well, those potatoes will not peel themselves. Back to work."

January 6, 433 AE, 12:30 on the Ministry Ship

Arliss sat across from the prime minister as they ate lunch in the private mess hall a couple of days after takeoff. He was glad Alex allowed him to bring his family along.

"Well," Alex had finished his last bite. "I would love to invite you and your family to my private quarters for dinner this evening. My wife would love to meet all of you. Justine is fitting into her role as the Galactic Federation's first lady rather well."

"That's good. I'll tell Marion. She'll be thrilled."

Arliss finished his last bite and stood up. "Well, I've got a lot of details to work out concerning the security upon arrival."

"Of course, no troubles so far?"

"Our scouts haven't picked up any movement from the Alliance."

"Good. Even if they do, we have a fleet backing us up."

"Yes." Arliss nodded. "Thank you for the lunch."

"Anytime."

Arliss made his way out of the mess hall and over to his office. The office was much larger than his office in the former job and still only half the size of his main office back at Olympic City. He sat down at the desk and picked up his data pad with the schematics for the landing pad on Earth. He swiped to the next page, which revealed the history of Earth.

Israel controlled most of Asia, all of Canada, most of the former United States, and most of Europe. Islam had all of Africa, most of the Americas, Australia, some of Europe, and a small part of Asia. Wars had been fought for years, but mostly the dispute was over one city known as Jerusalem. Both nations claimed Jerusalem for religious reasons. Alex planned on having the peace summit there on the ground, much to Arliss' dismay. With all the tension, he argued for having the summit on the Ministry High ship, but Alex would not have that.

Arliss set the pad down and remotely turned on the telecom across the room. "Call Marion."

His beautiful wife appeared on the screen.

"My, are you a sight for sore eyes." He smiled. "How is everyone?"

"They are doing fine. They are with their tutor right now and having a blast learning about the conflicts between Israel and Islam. The tensions between them are high, aren't they?"

"Yes. I have got my work cut out for me, and Alex has his. Speaking of Alex, he and Justine would like to have us over for dinner tonight."

"Oh, great. I cannot wait to meet them. Will you come home first?"

"Doubtful." He motioned to all the data pads on his desk. "I'll send you Justine's contact info, so you can get more details. How are you holding up?"

"Still getting used to this. The maids will not let me help with the chores. I am not sure what to do with myself."

"Well, perhaps Justine can help you with that."

"That's a good idea. Thanks, honey."

"Not a problem. Well, I have got to get back to work. I will see you tonight. I love you."

"I love you, too."

The screen went black, and Arliss looked at all the data pads on his desk and chuckled. His wife had too little to do, and he had the exact opposite problem.

CHAPTER SIX
February 10, 433 AE, 12:45

The long journey had been uneventful. Ethan and Elijah had remained undetected for so long. They were in the middle of the last evening shift before their day off. Ethan especially was looking forward to that as he served meatballs to another shipmate in line. He glanced farther down the line and suddenly his face turned white as a ghost. Ethan saw an old comrade, Billy Gosswick. He and Billy had served together in battle. He remembered the time he saved Billy's life during a battle on the planet Japan. Hopefully, his friend would not recognize him. Billy's uniform was that of the ministry guard. Then the moment Ethan dreaded came as the former comrade reached him and looked up. But the man did not seem to notice as Ethan put meatballs on his plate.

Just as Ethan thought he was clear, Billy stopped and looked back.

"Ethan Darkmoon! I cannot believe this. What are you doing here? I figured you would join the ministry guard."

"I decided to pursue far-uh-cooking." Ethan almost slipped up as he served another shipmate who moved around Billy

Billy took a step back to get out of the way of the others. "I can't believe this. Good to see you, buddy."

"You know this man?" A ministry lieutenant walked over to them from a table he had been sitting at. He was the same guard that had seen Ethan's fake ID on the way in.

"Yes, sir. This is Ethan Darkmoon, one of the best soldiers. Saved my life a couple of times."

"Well, according to his scan he is Titus Bartholomew and never served in the military."

Billy seemed confused. "Are you sure you read it right?"

"Perhaps I misread. Let me see your badge, son." The lieutenant reached over and pulled the badge Ethan had draped around his neck. He held the badge up and read aloud. "Titus Bartholomew. You do realize that using a fake ID on a ministry ship is treason?"

"Must have been given the wrong badge," Ethan smiled. "I'm sure we can get this sorted out."

"This has your picture on it!" The lieutenant motioned for four guards who stood at the door. The guards made their way over. "This man has a fake ID. Take him and his friend to a holding room."

"I'm sure this is just a big mix up." Billy tried to convince the lieutenant.

"Nevertheless, protocol must be followed. His friend, too." The lieutenant pointed farther down the line at Elijah. "They were traveling together."

Two of the guards grabbed Elijah, and they escorted both of them out of the mess hall and down the long hall through doors at the end, which led to the security office for that floor.

Ten Minutes Later

Arliss sat back in the chair in his office and relaxed. Most of the paperwork had been done for the day. He thought that civilian security paperwork was grueling. But as they said in the academy, everything was paperwork, and paperwork was everything.

The door slid open, and Lieutenant Mayfield walked in. "Sir, we have a situation."

Arliss leaned forward. "Okay."

"We found a couple of cooks with fake IDs."

"Drats! I knew we should have waited a few days to get the new security measures in place."

"I completely agree, sir. Unfortunately, our new prime minister is a bit eager."

"Well, I should have fought harder. Where are they?"

"Two different holding rooms. We figured we should separate them."

"Good idea." Arliss stood up. "What level? I'd like to conduct the interrogation."

"Level three."

Five Minutes Later

Arliss walked into the first holding room and found a young man with skin that was almost a bronze color. The only place he had seen that skin coloration was a picture of one of the Israelites on the ancestral home. He sat down across from the young man and picked up the info pad sitting on the table.

"Phillip Hancock, if that is your real name. Do you understand the charges facing you? And the severity of them?"

"Not entirely."

"Have you been living under a rock most of your life?" Arliss asked sarcastically.

"No. I have not been living under a rock. I was born in Vancouver on the Planet Washington."

"What is your real name and date of birth?"

"I am Elijah Darkmoon, and I was born on December 12, 432 AE.

Arliss chuckled. "Try again, buddy. That was a week before we took off on this journey. This is January 14, 433 AE. You are a fully grown man."

"I tell the truth," Elijah calmly insisted.

"It says here that there is no record of you. Did your parents break the law and have you outside of a medical facility?"

"Yes. I was born prematurely. They had no time."

"Still, there should have been some record. They should have brought you to the hospital and recorded your birth after the fact."

"No need. I was perfectly healthy. Please, it is important that I make my way to Israel."

"You can forget that. We are either going to send both of you out an airlock or place a deadly poison in your blood stream. If you give up your plan, we may give you a life sentence instead. So, what is it? Assassination attempt? Terrorist attack?"

"Neither. I must reach Israel. He has special plans for me."

"Who? Your father? What is his name?"

"He has many names. El Shaddai, Elohim, the Alpha and Omega, but more commonly as Jehovah."

"Jehovah? Are you with that cult, the Children of Jehovah?"

"I know of no such entity, but if they worship Jehovah, then they are indeed saints saved by grace. When the hour comes, the Lord will take them to be with him."

"What hour? Are you planning to kill them with a bomb?" Arliss became frantic.

"Only Jehovah knows the hour. He will come like a thief in the night, and they will rise up to meet him in the clouds."

Arliss stood up and stepped out where Mayfield waited. "What do you make of that?"

"Crazy talk. We have a few representatives of the Children of Jehovah on board. Perhaps we should place extra protection on them."

"Indeed," Arliss agreed. "Did they find anything in their quarters?"

"Negative. Just extra work uniforms."

"Does the other have a record?"

"Yes." Mayfield handed another info pad to Arliss. "His name is Ethan Darkmoon. He is twenty-five years old. Was given a few medals in the military. He was a marine and did qualify to become a ministry guard. He chose to move back and work on his grandfather's farm. His parents died in a mugging attack right after he was born. According to the DNA test, the other one would be twenty-two. There is no way they have the same parents. Cousins, perhaps?"

"Could be." Armed with new information, Arliss marched into the room on the other side of the hall and sat down across the table from Ethan.

Ethan looked up at him and asked. "Where is my friend? What have you done with him?"

"He's fine for now. A little messed up in the head, though. He thinks he is a few weeks old. He might be able to plead insanity but only if you tell us the truth. Let us start with your name, Ethan Darkmoon. Excellent service record in the military. I was a marine, too. Helped me pay for schooling. Why did you decline being in the ministry guard?"

"I like farming. Since my parents died, I stood to inherit all my grandfather's farm. As to Elijah's thoughts, I would not believe it if I did not see it myself. One day he was a small boy, and the next day he was a few years older. Every day it seems he ages more."

"And I'm supposed to believe this!" Arliss slammed the info pad down, stood up, and leaned forward with his hand on the table. Ethan did not budge. "Are you guys plotting an attack on the prime minister?"

"What?" Now Ethan was frightened. "No."

"The Children of Jehovah then?"

"No. We don't have any plans to do so. He just needs to reach Israel. My grandfather asked me to get him there. There's no assassination plot and no terrorist attack."

The door opened, and Mayfield motioned to Arliss. Reluctantly, Arliss walked out of the room, and the door slid shut behind him.

"What is it?" Arliss was a little agitated by the interruption.

"When we talked to the main representative of the Children of Jehovah, he said he wants to meet the one who goes by Elijah. Also, no bombs were discovered."

"Well, it's unconventional. Did he say why?"

"Not exactly. He was ecstatic though."

"I'm not sure. I'll talk to him."

"He's in the security waiting room."

Arliss made his way down the hall and through the sliding doors at the end. A short, bald man with the recognizable white robe sat in the waiting room. Unlike the others, his robe was lined with red. Arliss recognized him as High Priest Pierre Duval. Upon seeing Arliss, he stood up.

"High Priest Duval, I don't believe I've had the pleasure yet." They shook hands.

"Nor I, Chief Mars."

"Tell me, what is your fascination with this, Elijah?"

"What he spoke of is mentioned in our sacred text, the Holy Bible. In the book of Revelation, it speaks of the Rapture that will be followed by a great Tribulation."

"Rapture?" Arliss was confused.

"When Jesus Christ, the Messiah returns, all the believers who have accepted him as their Lord and Savior will be brought to Heaven—those who are alive and those who are dead. I understand the crimes against these two are punishable by death, and I would like to plead their cases and ask they be placed in our care."

"Unfortunately, I cannot myself break protocol, but I may speak to the prime minister on your behalf. You wished to speak to him."

"Yes. It is believed that the two witnesses will be the returned prophet, Elijah, and the hero, Moses, who led Israel out of slavery in Egypt."

"Mayfield," Mayfield joined Arliss from the hall, "Bring the High Priest to the holding cell to see this Elijah but remain with them at all times."

"Yes, sir." Mayfield followed Duval into the hall as the doors slid open for them.

Thirty Minutes Later

When Arliss entered the prime minister's office, Alex was seated behind his desk with his reading visors on and a huge stack of info pads in front of him. He looked up at the new chief and immediately stood up.

"Arliss?" He seemed delighted to see him. "Thank you for a much-needed break from the paperwork. I'm assuming this concerns the two that were taken into custody."

"Yes, sir. No bombs were found."

"Well, that's a relief." Alex sat back down. "I must admit I was a little worried."

"Me, too." Arliss nodded. "The High Priest Duval has requested me to see if you can delay their execution, if not cancel it and place them in their care. He believes the one with no record is of symbolic importance to his faith."

Alex stood up again and moved to the window. He looked out at a small nebula that the fleet was passing by. Then he turned back to his dear friend.

"As much as I would like to honor his request," he sighed, "I must decline. As a new prime minister, I need to show that I do not tolerate this kind of behavior and make a stern example. Execute both today. Airlock. Broadcast this to the whole network. On delay, of course, because we are too far from civilization."

"Agreed, sir."

Arliss felt wrong about this, but he decided that nothing would sway his good friend from changing his mind. He turned and walked out of the office.

One Hour Later

Arliss stood outside of the glass door and looked at the two men that awaited their cruel fate. Alex stood next to him on one side and on his other side stood Mayfield and a visibly distressed Duval. The high priest had tried with no avail to reason with the prime minister and had finally backed down and asked if he could at least be present."

Mayfield pressed a button, and the outer door opened. But for some reason Elijah and Ethan were not sucked out into space like they should have. "What is this?" Alex was stunned.

"I'm not sure, sir." Mayfield looked at the scanner. "The door is open, but they aren't being sucked out like they should. This is impossible."

"Is there a small force field around the door?"

"Negative. If there were a force field, they would still be sucked to the edge of the force field, at least. Also, the lack of oxygen would still kill them. They are showing no signs of a lack of oxygen. According to the scanner, no oxygen is in the room."

"They must have outside help or something." Alex shook his head.

"Jehovah's will." Duval smiled. "Nothing is impossible with Jehovah."

Alex shrugged. "Relock the door. Bring them to the injection chamber. We will poison them instead."

Fifteen Minutes Later

Arliss watched through the enforced glass as the doctors injected Ethan with the green poison. Quickly, Ethan began to suffocate, his face turned blue from a lack of oxygen, and he died on the table.

"See," Alex was relieved. "No interference there."

Then the doctor injected the poison into Elijah. But suddenly a cloud that was colored green left Elijah's body and entered the doctor and both security guards. All three of them ran toward the door in a state of panic as they began to suffocate. They fell toward the ground and were still.

Alex was infuriated. He punched the glass hard. "What is going on here? This man should be dead by now. The poison killed his friend. Why not him?"

Duval responded. "It is the power of Jehovah. Jehovah has plans for him to reach Israel. And the prophets Elijah and Moses won't be stopped by anyone."

Arliss could not believe what he had just seen. "Prepare the dead for burial and notify their families. But only their families, keep this information from spreading to the entire ship."

"Yes, sir." Mayfield motioned to the two guards next to them. "What do we do about the prisoner?"

"Good question." Arliss turned to the prime minister. "Databurt for your thoughts, friend."

"Put him in a cell for now. We'll try again when we get him to Earth."

Thirty-five Minutes Later

From his desk, Arliss watched Elijah in his cell through the telecom. Elijah seemed to show a bit of remorse for his friend as he sat on the metal slab that they called a bed. His bunkmate slept soundly on the other side of the room. Suddenly, Elijah stood up and moved to the center of the room. He got down on his knees, folded his hands, and bowed his head.

Arliss quickly turned the sound on.

Elijah began to speak, "Elohim, Father in Heaven. I pray that your mighty will be done. Forgive these unclean souls for they have no idea what power they are against. No idea at all."

"Stop your jabbering, fool." The cellmate awoke and sat up in his bed. "I'm trying to sleep."

"I must finish my prayer, kind sir." Elijah shook his head.

The man stood up and seized his roommate by the throat but suddenly he let go, got back in bed and fell asleep.

"Jehovah, you are so powerful and full of love. I pray that more souls come to know you before your hour arrives. In your Holy Name. Amen."

Arliss could not believe that yet again this man seemed to be protected by a supernatural force. Just then Mayfield appeared on the screen.

"What is it now?" Arliss stood up.

"Sir, one of our accompanying ships has picked up an escape pod that is of Asiatic design. It holds one person who says he was held prisoner aboard an Asiatic war vessel but managed to escape."

"Where were they headed?"

"The ancestral home."

Arliss was fully alert now. "Have you alerted the military vessels?"

"Yes. They are on high alert. Scouts have picked up an entire fleet only a day behind us."

"Has the prime minister been alerted?"

"Yes."

"What is the prisoner's name?"

"He calls himself Moses."

CHAPTER SEVEN
February 12, 433 AE, 09:17

The fact that the prisoner without records and the person who escaped the Asiatic-Russian Alliance went by the names of the two witnesses had not escaped Arliss' attention. *Could that really be a coincidence?* He thought, as the new chief of ministry security stood next to General Hayden on the bridge.

The entire fleet had gathered around the planet Earth. Alex stood a way behind them. The prime minister had seen combat before he went to school, so he knew how to hide his nervousness.

"How close are they, Lieutenant?" Hayden asked the comm officer.

She replied promptly, "They are twenty minutes from firing range, sir."

"How many of them are there?" Arliss was curious.

"My sensors are detecting five!" she responded.

"We have more ships." The general was confident. "Higher class, too. They are no match at all."

The five Asiatic-Russian ships dropped out of hyper speed. Then another, and another and another. The ships kept coming like wildfire!

Arliss had an awfully bad feeling about this. Five ships they could handle, but ships continued to appear out of nowhere. He looked around and saw the horrified looks on the faces of his comrades.

"Sir, there are two hundred ships and counting. One is hailing us."

"Hide the prime minister!" Arliss commanded the two guards that accompanied him. "Do not leave his side."

The enemy could not know that the leader of the Galactic Federation was on board. If they got a hold of him, the fallout would be disastrous.

The guards followed Alex through the doors to his office. As soon as the doors slid shut, the comm officer accepted the call, and General Wong appeared on the screen.

"General Hayden, I presume. You are outnumbered and outgunned. Surrender the planet to us, and we will let you leave in peace. If not, we will blow you out of the sky."

"General Wong, you are violating the peace agreement that was made two years ago. Do you really want to risk another war?"

"This won't be a war. It will be a slaughter, and we will have one great hostage. You do not have to hide your prime minister any longer."

"I'm not sure what you are talking about."

"Don't play games with me, General Hayden. I have sources on your ship who have told me the prime minister is on board."

"Your sources are wrong. We will not back down. Leave now and spare your Empire the cost of a war with the Galactic Federation."

"That was the only warning! We will destroy you!"

The screen went blank.

"How soon will they be in firing range?" Hayden asked.

"A few minutes, sir." The comm officer was visibly shaken.

Suddenly, one of the Asiatic-Russian ships exploded with no cause. Then another and another. Ship after ship began to spontaneously self-destruct.

"What in tarnation is going on?" The general was stunned.

Arliss and all the officers watched in amazement as the space in front of them filled with the flames of exploding ships. After three astounding minutes, the flames dissipated and not a single ship was left intact, except for the other Federation ships.

For a while no one could say anything. Alex staggered from the office. He looked at the debris that remained, shocked. "What happened?"

"They all self-destructed." Arliss finally managed to get the words out. "I'm not sure how to explain this. It is crazy. I wouldn't believe it if I hadn't seen it for myself."

"Me, neither." General Hayden shook his head in disbelief.

Two Hours Later

Moses and Elijah sat in their cells across from each other, both facing the wall. Elijah's cellmate was still fast asleep. Then, as one, they rose and moved to the front of the cells. The guard noticed the movement but was not concerned. The force fields would keep them in.

In a flash, both force fields disappeared. Moses and Elijah emerged from their cells.

"Hey!" The surprised guard almost dropped his blast rifle as he grabbed the weapon and aimed it at them. "Don't move. Stay right there."

All at once, the guard felt overwhelmingly tired. He fell to his knees and then lay down on the floor and fell fast asleep. The doors to the waiting room opened before them, letting them out. The two guards, who normally stood at the door, and the security woman at the desk had fallen into a deep sleep. The two prisoners exited the room without hesitation. As they passed through the hallway, any nearby soldiers drowsily stumbled to the ground. It was as if the swiftness of their footsteps had set off an intangible domino effect that only they were immune to. Mayfield walked out of the mess hall. Seeing the prisoners, he reached for his weapon but collapsed before he could draw. He slumped against the wall and slid down to the floor, overcome with exhaustion.

Thirty Minutes Later

Arliss sat at his desk, the last few moments racing through his mind. The Alliance had them dead to rights but then all opposing ships appeared to self-destruct without any warning. He looked down at the desk and noticed the data pad that Duval had given him. He picked the pad up and looked at the menu. A list of each book in the Children of Jehovah's religious text was displayed on the screen. Arliss swiped to the bottom of the list and found a book titled *Revelation*.

He pressed on that label, and the text appeared on the screen. He began to read. The book was confusing, full of apocalyptic symbolism. It described a period of tribulation that would precede the coming of Jesus Christ. According to Duval, one sect believed the Rapture would come before the tribulation, but the other sect believed that he would come during the middle. The scripture told of a mark with which people could buy, sell, and own things, including property. One section stood out to him. He reread it several times, trying to make sense of the prophecy.

> A third angel followed them and said in a loud voice: "If anyone worships the beast and its image and receives its mark on their forehead or on their hand, they, too, will drink the wine of God's fury, which has been poured full strength into the cup of his wrath. They will be tormented with burning sulfur in the presence of the holy angels and of the Lamb. And the smoke of their torment will rise for ever and ever. There will be no rest day or night for those who worship the beast and its image, or for anyone who receives the mark of its name." This calls for patient endurance on the part of the people of God who keep his commands and remain faithful to Jesus.

Arliss was still confused, but he could see that this mark would be trouble for those against the so-called Antichrist.

What am I doing? He suddenly put the book down. Then he remembered all the recent events. People used to be passive aggressive and simply ignored the Children of Jehovah. But now they were overly aggressive and more violent than he had ever seen. That, along with the failed execution attempts of Elijah, the arrival of Moses, and now the completely and unexplained annihilation of the Asiatic-Russian fleet could not be a mere coincidence.

He was about to take up the pad up again when the door opened, and a guard rushed in. "Sir, we have an emergency."

"What's going on?" Arliss stood up.

"The prisoners are gone."

"Which prisoners?" Arliss was almost afraid to ask.

"Elijah and Moses. They took an escape pod and went to the planet. They landed somewhere close to Jerusalem."

Arliss pounded his fist on the desk. "How could this happen? We have the best security in the galaxy."

"Sir," The guard was reluctant. "They fell asleep."

"Asleep? Are you telling me that the best security guards around, most of whom are ex-military, fell asleep?"

"Yes, sir. Including the soldiers and cooks in the mess hall. According to surveillance, only the force fields in their cells failed. As they walked, anyone they encountered collapsed in a fit of exhaustion. Even Mayfield. They are waking up now."

"Question all of them. Find out what happened."

"Yes, sir." The guard turned and rushed out.

Arliss collapsed back into his seat and shook his head in disbelief. It was just another event in a series of events that could not be explained.

Something powerful was at work. Could this Jehovah really exist? Could this be the beginning of the end?

Seven Hours Later

Alex Harper stood by the window in his office, a glass of wine in his hand. He thought about the events that occurred earlier that day. He could possibly explain the failed attack from the Alliance. Somehow, system failure had caused all their ships to self-destruct. However, the doctors and engineers could not explain the failed execution attempts. Maybe if he just let the prisoner go to Israel and made the evidence of the failed attempts disappear, it would be for the best. If this got out, it would be a huge embarrassment for his administration.

"Alex."

"Who's there?" Alex turned and looked around the room but could not see anyone.

The lights suddenly went dark.

Alex set his glass down on the table. "I asked who is there? This room is off limits."

He heard a faint laughter, and then the room glowed with a strange red light and became foggy. A dark figure in a black cloak appeared in the middle of the room. The figure stood over seven feet tall. From under the hood, Alex saw evil-looking eyes that appeared to be on fire.

"Who are you?" Alex yelled in terror. "Someone help!"

"They can't hear you, but I am not here to harm you. I'm here to offer you complete dominion."

"What?" Alex backed up again. "How can I trust you? I don't even know who you are."

"My name is Lucifer. I have dominion over the spirit realm in this form of existence, and I can offer you complete dominion over the physical realm—not just the Federation but the Alliance and beyond. You could control all the stars farther than the eye can see and bring peace to the universe. You can have all the riches at your disposal. Everyone will fear and worship you. Forget being prime minister. You can be a god."

"I can have all that power? What do I have to do?"

"Just accept my offer, and you will know what to do."

"I accept. Give me this power."

Alex felt his chest tighten and fell to the ground in immense pain. He cried out with pain and scratched at the floor. Helpless, he curled up into the fetal position and blacked out. Lucifer disappeared, and the lights returned to normal moments before Arliss walked in. He rushed over to his friend and got onto his knees as the prime minister woke up.

"Are you all right, sir?"

"Yes." He let Arliss help him to his feet. "I'm not sure what happened. Why are you here?"

"The prisoners escaped. Both Elijah and Moses. A crew is preparing to go after them. Are you sure you are fine?"

"Yes. Forget the prisoners. I'd rather have the failed executions be swept under the rug."

"Are you sure, sir?" Arliss was concerned.

"Yes. But we need to prepare to go down to the planet. I want to sign a treaty with Israel as soon as possible. I need to start work on my security plan."

"What do you mean?"

"We need to place a mark on everyone. Without it, they cannot buy or sell anything, nor can they own property."

Two Hours Later

Arliss could not believe what he had heard Alex speaking about. If the texts were correct, then the prime minister could be the Antichrist, not just the prime minister, but a good friend. As he sat on his living room couch and took a sip from his glass of water, he felt tears start to form in his eyes. He heard the door slide open and quickly tried to wipe the tears away as he set his glass down.

Travis came in and sat down next to him.

"What's wrong?"

"I can't fool you, can I?" Arliss laughed slightly. "Just my friend isn't who I thought he was. Do you know anything about the end times prophesied in that text?"

"A little. What do you want to know?"

"When this Jesus returns, is that it?"

"Well, most of us believe that there will be a second chance for those who don't accept the mark of the beast, but times will be very tough for them. But with Jehovah on their side, they can get through anything, like when he healed Mother. If what we want is his will, then our needs will be met. He gives us not necessarily what we want, but what he knows we need. He doesn't control everything in our lives, but he can use all situations to draw us closer to him."

"You were always a good student, weren't you?" Arliss let out a smile.

"Learned from the best."

The proud father reached out his hand to touch his son. But instead, he stood up with a start. His son was no longer there. His clothes remained in a pile on the couch. "Travis!" Arliss grabbed his son's clothes up in his hands and felt them, still warm.

"What's wrong?" His wife raced out of the hall in a hurry. She stopped and sighed. "Did he leave his clothes out again?"

Then she noticed the horrified expression on his face.

"He . . . he was right here." Arliss began to shake. "He was sitting right here with these clothes on him. Now he's not here."

Marion moved over to him. "Are you okay? You're not making any sense."

Arliss began to breathe heavily, and then he felt a sharp pain in his chest. He dropped the clothes and fell to the ground. The last thing he saw was his wife rushing toward him as he blacked out.

Somewhere Between the BC and AD Timelines

The temple was dark, and the air was tense as evening set in. The crowd gathered on the steps and waited as the Roman ruler took a long pause. The decision was a tough one. He glanced down at the man under guard. This prisoner had truly done no wrong in his opinion, but the crowd and religious leaders disagreed. They said his lies would light a flame and bring about a rebellion that could threaten the Roman Empire. The commander knew they were exaggerating because of their prejudice toward this man, who claimed to be a savior to the Jews. He was not a warrior, like most Jews had thought, but a man of peace who is said to have performed miraculous deeds, someone who challenged their authority.

Finally, the other prisoner was brought out by two more guards. The ruler gave a sigh of relief. This prisoner was the scum of the city, a thief and a murderer, who just last week the people cheered at his capture and mocked him at his trial. The crowd would surely choose him over the first man to keep locked up. They rejoiced when the first prisoner had reached Jerusalem.

The great commander stepped forward and cleared his voice to speak. "Today we follow a familiar tradition! You get to pick one of these two prisoners to release. Who do you choose?"

A couple of people shouted, "Barabbas! Barabbas! Barabbas!" More followed, until the whole crowd had joined in, "Barabbas! Barabbas! Barabbas! Barabbas!"

The leader was troubled. He looked at both prisoners and reluctantly nodded. The guards released the second man, who quickly disappeared into the crowd.

The leader knew he had to appease the religious rulers in order to maintain control of the people. He looked again at the prisoner, with a disdain for what he was about to say.

"Crucify him!"

The helpless man was dragged out to the middle of the crowd and chained to two stakes. The guards stripped him of his clothes and began to whip him fiercely. The whips came down over and over. The leader could hear the whips ripping at the flesh and see the blood that flowed from the man's wounds into a large puddle on the ground. After a few minutes, the man was unrecognizable. The only feature that separated him from a beast was his long hair and beard that were covered in blood.

The saddened commander almost cried at the sight before him. He finally had had enough. The crowd also became silent after realizing what they had chosen. A couple of the guards were whipping with looks of horror on their faces.

"Stop!" he shouted, "Bring the cross."

While two guards carried the cross toward the victim, one guard produced a crown made of thorns and placed it on the prisoner's head. The two other guards forced the prisoner to pick up the heavy cross and drag it toward a hill off in the distance. The leader knew that was common practice, so he could not stop it, but as the prisoner fell for a third time, he saw a chance to help. He pointed at a man in the crowd.

"You there!"

The man came forward.

"Help him!"

The newcomer did not hesitate. He rushed to the prisoner's aid and helped carry the cross to the top of the hill as everyone followed closely. Once at the site, the newcomer rejoined the crowd, and the guards lifted the beaten man onto the cross. They positioned him with his arms outstretched on the side beams and the rest of his body on top of the main beam. The man screamed as they nailed his hands and feet to the wooden instrument of death. The guards used ropes to pull the cross upright and dropped the bottom of the cross into a newly dug hole so that it would remain standing. Above the man's head was a sign that read: Here lies Jesus of Nazareth. King of the Jews.

The man looked down at the crowd and to the supreme figures. To their surprise, he managed to shout.

"Father, why have you forsaken me?"

"He's calling for Elijah!" One guard mocked him, "Let's see if Elijah comes to save him."

For what seemed like hours, the man held on. Two other men who were on crosses on either side of him seemed to be interested in him. One spoke.

"You who are going to destroy the temple. Come down and save yourself if you are truly the Son of God."

"Don't you fear God?" the other criminal shouted across to the other. "We are punished justly for our actions. But this man is innocent." He paused and looked up at the man between them. "Jesus, please remember me when you come into your kingdom."

Jesus looked at the offender and replied, "Truly I tell you, today you will be with me in paradise." He looked up at the sky and shouted, "Father! Forgive them! For they do not know what they are doing!"

An hour later, the brutalized savior looked up at the sky again. "It is finished!"

His head dropped forward, and he died.

No sooner had that occurred, the earth began to shake violently. The crowd turned to see the temple falling into pieces and tumbling to the ground with people fleeing from it, some trampled over others in a fit of panic.

The powerful leader shook his head in disbelief. He looked over at the guard next to him. Not knowing his leader's eyes were on him, the guard looked up at Jesus and spoke,

"Surely this man was the Son of God."

CHAPTER EIGHT

February 12, 433 AE, 20:47, Olympic City, Planet Washington,

New Chief of Civilian Security Miles Javers stood where the former chief would stand at the train station and looked down as the crowd began to dissipate. The prime minister was clear before the ship left; he wanted the Children of Jehovah to be locked up. *"No tolerance for their blasphemy"* is what Alex Harper had said.

Javers wondered if Mars knew about the change in policy regarding the overzealous scum. He did not really care if the last chief knew or not. He gave a slight grin as a group made their way out of a dark alley in their white robes. They stood in the center of the station, raised their hands in the air, and began to say a prayer.

Javers got on the radio, "All units, move in."

"Are you sure about . . ."

"Yes! I'm sure!" He hated being questioned like that. "Move in."

The guards surrounded the group, and Javers rode the escalator down to meet them. He came out just as they finished the prayer. He grabbed his radio again and patched through to the announcement system. "This is Chief Javers of the civilian security. These public demonstrations are now illegal. Leave now or face prosecution."

"We are not breaking any laws, sir." A young man who was rather tall and had red hair stepped forward. "We are about spreading Jehovah's love and peace."

Javers grabbed his laser prodder and zapped the man, who keeled over onto his knees for a moment, and then stood back up.

The man pleaded. "The prime minister promised us change."

The stern chief smirked, "He never said it would be for the better. Arrest them all."

As the officers started to move in, Javers noticed his wife among them. He turned toward her with what appeared to be love in his eyes. He held out his hand and began to plead, "Come back to me, and I will not arrest you with the others, my sweet Jasmine."

She pulled away from him and shook her head. "I cannot support your actions, but you can change and join us."

With that, Javers angrily pulled his laser prodder back out of its sheath and grabbed her. At that moment, all members of the Children of Jehovah vanished. Their empty robes fluttered to the ground. A few officers had vanished as well.

Javers, suddenly empty handed, lost his balance and fell to the ground on top of her robe. He quickly pulled himself up, trying to regain composure. As he did, a woman began to scream. He turned to see her frantically running around next to her baby's stroller.

"Where is my baby? My baby!"

Javers rushed over to her. "Calm down, miss."

He peered into the stroller and saw baby clothes and a blanket but no baby. In an instant, the rest of the crowd began to panic. One man grabbed an officer by the collar.

"What's going on here? Where's my wife?"

Another officer approached Javers. "What do we do, sir?"

"I've got an idea." He patched his radio through the announcement system again. "Due to some unforeseen circumstances, I am issuing a curfew for all nonemergency personnel. Everyone return to their homes. All businesses will be closed. Report any missing persons to your local security headquarters as soon as you return home." The crowd was not listening, though. "Anyone found not complying will face prosecution and possible fines."

The crowd did not dissipate. In fact, it grew larger by the minute.

"Guards! Use force! We need to put a stop to this now!"

One guard used his laser prodder to zap the man who had grabbed him. Two more people rushed him angrily.

Javers realized then what he had to do. He grabbed his other radio. "Civilian Chief to Commander Matthews."

"Matthews here."

"We need military support here in Olympic City," Javers requested.

"Try to hang on. Riots are breaking out all over the planet. Actually, all over the Federation—all the planets."

"All of them?" Javers was dumbfounded.

"Yes. We don't want them to know this yet." Commander Matthews told him.

A woman appeared on the large telecom screen on the side of a nearby building.

"This is Cynthia Blackwell reporting. Several disappearances have occurred over the entire federation, and the citizens are demanding answers. This may possibly be a terrorist attack by the Asiatic-Russian Alliance."

Javers grabbed an officer. "Go find that woman and order her to stop the cast before it spreads."

"Copy that, sir." The officer raced away.

Around the Same Time, an Apartment in Olympic City, Planet Washington

Andrew Larkendome sat on his couch, watching a futbol game on the screen. He could not help but think about the fact that his daughter had decided to join that wretched cult. He wondered if the new policies in place would allow him to stop her. He would find out the next morning when the policies were officially announced.

The newscaster stood up and cheered as his team's star player, Marcus Sunstopper, rushed toward the goal with only two defenders left in the way. The first defender tried a slide, but the great athlete dodged him and then darted past the second, on toward the goal.

"Yes!" Andrew shouted enthusiastically, jumping up from the couch. "This is your moment, Sunstopper!" But just as Sunstopper got close to the goal, he vanished, leaving his uniform in a pile on the grass as the ball rolled past the stunned goalkeeper and into the goal. A few other players and several fans disappeared as well.

"What the heck?" Andrew sat back down and stared blankly at the screen.

The announcer spoke up. "What is going on here? It appears that some people in the stands and on the field have completely vanished, Craig." He turned, but his colleague was not there next to him. Only Craig's suit was there in his chair. "Craig! Oh geez! What is happening here?"

Suddenly, a woman appeared on the screen, interrupting with a breaking news program.

"This is Cynthia Blackwell reporting. Several disappearances have occurred over the entire Federation, and people are demanding answers. This may possibly be a terrorist attack by the Asiatic-Russian Alliance. Most of those who disappeared were toddlers, infants, and those who are members of the Children of Jehovah. This is happening all over the Federation planets." She paused, listening to her headset. "And now reports have just come in about disappearances within the Asiatic-Russian Alliance as well."

Andrew shook his head. He knew this was serious, but there was nothing he could do. Security had ordered a curfew. He wondered how he should explain to his daughter what was going on. Then it hit him, and he shot straight up out of his chair, spilling his beer. Paying it no mind, he rushed across to the stairs.

"Grace!"

He flew up the stairs like he was as light as a feather and barely let the door slide open, bursting into her room and running over to her bed. To his horror, his fears were confirmed. Her abandoned nightgown was tucked under the covers. He fell to the ground and let the tears pour out. He remembered his wife. She had been killed in action a few years ago. And now his Gracie!

He got up and solemnly walked out of the room. As he did, he heard a beep at his door. He descended the stairs and opened the front door to see two officers.

One officer spoke up. "Sir, given the tragedy that has unfolded, we are checking all houses. Has anyone in your house disappeared?"

"My daughter, Grace Larkendome."

He wrote her name down on his data pad. "What about your wife?"

"She was already deceased."

"Okay, sir. We will remind you that a curfew is in place until you are told otherwise."

"Of course."

As the officers moved on, Andrew shut the door and returned to Grace's room. He saw the data pad on her bed stand. It had been given to her by that cult. He picked the pad up, sat on her bed, and began to read.

February 13, 433 AE, 08:00; Same Apartment

After hours and hours of reading, Andrew could not hide from the truth. He had skipped over some pieces but got the gist of this. This Jehovah did indeed exist. He created everything—all the planets and the stars, the mountains, the oceans, and every living thing. When sin entered the world, mankind was plagued by darkness. God tried to rid the plague with a great flood, but sin was still in all mankind, even the faithful ones that he spared from the rising waters. So, he devised a plan for redemption. He sent his Son, Jesus, to Earth as a man. Jesus died on the cross for the sins of everyone, and any who believes in him and accepts God's Holy Spirit into their hearts would be favored in the eternal judgment. In the end times, they would be taken to be with Jesus in heaven. Those who remained would have a second chance.

Andrew stood up and walked over to his daughter's window. He looked up at the two light blue moons. Getting onto his knees, he placed the pad on the windowsill and his hands on the pad.

Closing his eyes, he began to pray.

"Jehovah, my Heavenly Father. I have read your word. I honestly believe all of it. I believe you sent your Son to pay the price for all of us on that cross. I am willing to do your will. Please send your Holy Spirit into my heart and show me what your will is. Fill me with your wisdom and understanding. Help me guide others to know you as well. In your Son's righteous name, Amen."

Andrew went back downstairs, carrying the pad with him. He turned on his telepad and waited for an answer.

Chief Javers appeared on the screen. "Andrew. Your office must be busy now with the news that is spiraling. How can I help you?"

"I need special permission to break curfew. I want to do a story, but I have a specific location in mind."

"Where?"

"One of the underground sanctuaries that belong to that cult. Do you know of any?"

"Yes. I'll send a couple of my officers to pick you up."

"Thank you, friend."

"Anything for you."

One Hour Later

Andrew Larkendome stood at the entrance to the large underground hall. There were about forty rows of pews on either side. Half-way down the middle of the rows was an aisle crossing the main aisle and the two aisles on the side. Each aisle was covered with a red rug that was lined with gold. At the front of the room was a platform with red carpet. The rug from the main aisle went up the five steps to the top where a pulpit stood. Behind the pulpit, a cross was hung against the back wall. The walls on the side were lined with mosaic portraits. The sun shined through the mosaic icons on the back wall.

"Is this what you had in mind, sir?" One of the two officers behind him interrupted the silence.

"Yes. This will be perfect. Is the crew almost here?"

"Yes, sir."

The back doors slid open, and two men came in carrying bags of equipment and a small recording device that looked like a small black box with a glass circle in the middle. "Set the camera just a couple of feet before the stage. I will be standing at the pulpit."

"Yes, sir." The grunts moved forward and started to set up the stand.

Andrew ascended the steps to the stage and walked around the podium, preparing to address the camera. As he took his place behind the podium, the back doors slid open again and in walked Cynthia Blackwell.

"So, Andrew, where do you want me to do this story? On top of the podium? That is perfect, actually." She approached down the main aisle but stopped when Andrew began to laugh. "I think you are confused, Cynthia. I am doing this story. While I think you are great at your job, the message I have can only be told clearly by me."

"Oh." She paused. "I'm sorry. I just assumed."

"That's quite alright."

"We are ready, sir." One of the grunts, who was incredibly young, turned on the recording device. "We are live in three, two, one . . ."

"People of the Federation, you may know me by my professional name, Flash Casey. But I will now identify my given name, Andrew Larkendome. Given recent events where a few million people have disappeared, including all known members of the Children of Jehovah and all toddlers and infants, I have taken it upon myself to study their text. I have drawn the conclusion that they were in fact correct, that there is an all-powerful entity, and his name is Jehovah. He created the whole universe by simply willing it into existence. If you really look around at the beauty of nature, you can see that there is an intelligent designer behind all of this. He has now taken those who believe up to be with him in heaven. But hope is not lost for us that remain, for those who repent of their sins and accept his Holy Spirit into their hearts will be saved. They will live in the millennial reign of Christ.

But we must beware, for there is one who will deceive us. The Antichrist will make a treaty with Israel. He will make it mandatory to wear his mark on their foreheads or right hands. No one can buy or sell anything without this mark, nor can they own property. This is a dark day while the Antichrist reigns. But rest assured, his reign will be short. For Jesus, the same Jesus who died on the cross for our sins, will return with an army. He will defeat the Antichrist and will rule the universe for a thousand years. Come here to the Church at 612 Antioch Drive, and I will show you the way."

"Done." The oldest grunt turned off the device.

"What was that garbage?" Cynthia laughed. "What kind of game are you playing, Flash?"

"Call me Andrew. Flash is gone."

"You're not serious. You don't actually believe that do you?"

"Yes, I do. Open your eyes, Cynthia. The truth is all around us. There is no other logical explanation."

"Forget it. I'm out of here." Cynthia turned abruptly and walked down the hall out of the church.

The younger grunt left with Cynthia, but the older grunt stepped forward. "I lost my wife in these vanishings. Please, tell me more."

"I have to admit, I am learning this as I go." Andrew took a pad out of his bag and handed it to him. "This is a copy of the text. I suggest reading Genesis of the Old Testament and Matthew and Revelation of the New Testament."

The grunt sat down and began to read. As he did, Andrew saw an old book with paper pages on the podium. He opened it and realized that it was a copy of the original text. Not all of them had been destroyed after all.

CHAPTER NINE

February 10, 433 AE, 08:47 Earth Time (ET), New Delhi, India, Islamic State, Earth

Aaqil Khaleel stood in the middle of the living room with a disgusted look on his face. His heart felt different. Inside was a deep sadness, but he knew what had to be done. The Islamic State had made it clear that those who disobeyed the law and converted to another religion would be executed.

He looked down at his daughter, Mahja, as she sat on the couch with a look of terror on her face. On the table in front of her sat a large book. The title of the book: *The Holy Bible.*

This was clearly the sacred text of the Messianic Jews, the sworn enemy of the Islamic State. If she had converted to Buddhism, her death would be swift and without pain because the Buddhists make up less than one percent of the population. But conversion to Messianic Judaism meant that she was a national traitor, and they would make an example of her.

He looked over to the kitchen where his wife sat on the floor, sobbing a great deal. He wanted so much to join her, but he knew if he should show weakness, Mahja would think she was right in her choice. Then came the dreaded knock on the door.

The troubled father slowly made his way over to the door and swung it open. Two guards stood in the door with black tunics on their heads and white robes. Aaqil motioned them in with his head, and they moved past him and stopped next to his terrified daughter. At that moment he thought of a quick escape for her. One final chance.

"We just bought this house. The book might not be hers," he lied.

He remembered walking in on her when she was reading from the wretched black book.

"Is this your book?" One of the men asked her.

"Yes. It is."

Aaqil's heart sank further. "You stupid girl! Who has turned you against us?"

"Give us a name and the book, and we will offer you a quick death," the man spoke again.

She stood up, picked the book up and handed the book to the man.

"Who is the one who turned you?"

"Jehovah."

"And where is this Jehovah?"

Mahja silently pointed up.

"On the roof? This house has no stairs to the roof."

"Not on the roof. Heaven." Mahja Replied.

The second man put the book in a black bag that hung around his shoulder. Then both men grabbed her and pulled her out of the house. She did not scream at all. They threw her onto the ground amid a crowd. Most of the crowd began to chant.

"Almawt! Almawt! Almawt!"

They stripped her of most of her clothing and began to whip her tirelessly. After five minutes, they stopped, and one guard pulled her to her feet. He drew his large, curved blade. As the guard prepared to swing the sharp instrument of death, Aaliq saw his daughter look up at the sky and smile. She shouted out with great joy.

"Jehovah! I knew you would come!"

The guard swung his sword, but as he swung, Mahja disappeared. What remained of her clothes fell to the ground, and the guard toppled over. He quickly stood up as the shouting stopped. The crowd stood with fearful eyes, barely moving. Aaliq wanted to run out to the spot, but he thought better of it. He turned to see his wife who stood behind him with the same surprised look on her face. The surprised father shut the door and sat on the couch. He put his hands over his head and cried, "What have I done? What have I done!"

February 12, 433 AE, 12:34 E.T., Islamidab (formerly New York City), Islamic State, Earth

President Omar sat in his office. He watched on the televised screen that hung across the room. Several prisoners were lined up for beheading. Most of them were converts to Messianic Judaism, few were converts to Buddhism, but one or two were murderers. He watched as the first in line, a Buddhist convert, was forced to his knees. A guard swung his sword, and the head fell off. As the guard moved on to the next prisoner, almost all the rest of the prisoners vanished into thin air, leaving only their clothes behind.

The shocked ruler jumped out of his chair as the crowd and prisoners began to panic. He noticed that all the prisoners that disappeared were converts to Messianic Judaism. The door to his office burst open and in rushed his media consultant.

"Sir, given the event and other similar events, what we should tell the media?"

"Change records." The president was in a state of panic. "Tell them those that disappeared were Israeli spies and not necessarily converts. We can't have them believing that everything we stand for is wrong."

"Yes, sir." The man left again in just as quick a manner as he had come.

Omar sat back down and hit rewind on the security monitor to watch the event again. There had been no sign of tampering, and no sign of anyone working behind the scenes to cause this. He wondered how someone could go to such extravagant measures to disprove Islam.

February 13, 433 AE, 00:34 FT (Federation Time), Medical Bay, Ministry Ship, Earth's Orbit

Arliss woke up slowly. He lay still as his eyes came into focus. He realized he was in a medical room in the hospital deck. He looked to his side and saw Marion as she sat in her chair with her head leaned back against a pillow. She was barely awake. She glanced over at him and quickly leaned forward. She gently held his hand.

"You're awake. I was so worried."

"What happened?"

"You had a heart attack."

Then the last memory flooded back into Arliss' head. "Travis. Did that . . ."

Tears started to well up in her eyes and she nodded. "Yeah. He is gone. He is not the only one. Duval, over 75 percent of the Israelites, and a few of the Muslims that converted to the Israelites religion. A couple of your guards, too. Alex signed a peace treaty with Israel that grants them full control of Jerusalem but allows the Muslims to come and go as well. The disappearances did not just occur here. They occurred everywhere. All members of the Children of Jehovah are gone. Doc said you need to take it easy, but you should recover fine. Oh, Alex will want to know you're awake." She stood up and kissed him on the lips. "He's been very worried. I'll go tell a doctor and let him know."

She walked out of the room, and Arliss looked up at the ceiling. He knew that the religious text spoke of event, such as the signing of a treaty and the disappearances. They were all prophesied. Then he remembered hearing Alex's plan of a mark. He continued to look up and began to pray.

"God, if you are there, please show me what to do. Help me make sense of this all. Show me a sign that you are real."

Then a figure appeared by his bed. He saw Travis. His son smiled at him and then spoke a warning, "Beware the mark."

Just as quickly as he had appeared, Travis disappeared again.

"Travis. Come back!" He sat up, but a couple of nurses rushed in and held him back while one of them sedated him.

> **Note to reader:** From here on, I will always use Federation time so sometimes might appear to be in the evening but are not if they are on Earth because Earth time is two days and twelve hours behind Federation time.

February 13, 433 AE, 10:15 FT, Jerusalem, Islamic State, Earth

Aphra Qasim stood in the window of her apartment and watched the riots from the TV. People were punching at law enforcement officers, vandalizing property, and throwing glass bottles. The officers were trying to gain control using tear gas and knife-sticks, but the crowd was too large.

She wanted to call and see if her parents were all right. But she knew her father was smart enough to stay inside during these dangerous times. She had slept in because this was her day off from her editing job but was startled awake with the sound of an explosion. Her husband had left the TV on when he left for work at the embassy. The news said that those who disappeared were Israeli spies. But she recognized one of the men who disappeared as a former colleague who had tried to convert her to Christianity. The people did not seem to be buying that story, either.

At that moment, her phone rang.

"Hello, father, is that you?" she asked, eagerly pressing the receiver to her ear.

"Yes, dear. I wanted you to know that your mother and I are safe."

"Praise Allah." She closed her eyes for a few seconds. "I was worried about you."

"I'm not sure he's the one to praise, my sweet daughter"

"What do you mean, Father? And what about Mahja?"

"Mahja converted to Christianity."

"What? Are you sure?"

"I caught her reading their sacred text. That is not all. She disappeared, too."

Aphra sat down on the chair and slowly began to cry. "You think this is the Christian Rapture, don't you?"

"Yes, my child." He was confident. "There is no other logical explanation. Your mother and I think we need to leave here as soon as possible. We have arranged for a flight to Jerusalem. Can you see if your husband can prepare a safe trip to the airport for us? As a diplomat, he has friends of high power."

"Yes, I will," she agreed.

"It is probably best to not let him know what we think about the president's story."

"I understand, Father. I will go to the embassy now. I will pray for your safety." Aphra hung up the phone.

After a moment of silence, she pulled her red tunic up over her face and grabbed her purse. Making her way across the room, she opened the door and tapped the guard on the shoulder. "I'm heading to the embassy to see my husband."

The guard nodded and led her through the hall and down the stairs into the parking garage. They made their way over to a white limousine, and he opened the back door for her. She stepped into car, and the guard shut the door.

February 13, 433 AE, 10:30 ET, Jerusalem, Islamic State, Earth

Aphra walked into the Islamic embassy, which was a small, two-story building right across from the site where the Israelis were rebuilding their ancient temple. The temple was almost complete, thanks to technology from the Galactic Federation. She ascended the stairs with the guard right behind her. She opened the office door and walked in. Her husband, Abdul, sat behind his desk. Upon her entrance, he stood up as the guard closed the door behind them.

"My beautiful wife. Have you heard about the riots starting throughout our territories?"

"Yes, Abdul." She came around the desk, and they hugged. "My parents wish to visit us, and I wanted to see if you can arrange for a safe transport for them to the airport."

"Of course. You know you could have called on the phone."

"Yes. But this gives me an excuse to see you. Plus, I have some shopping to do."

"Well, it is truly a delight." He kissed her on the forehead. "I will make the arrangements. Then I have a meeting with leaders from the Galactic Federation. The disappearances have not just happened here. They have happened all over the known universe."

"What!" She shook her head in disbelief. "What about here? The Israelis lost over four-fifths of their population. It is very worrisome. Will your sister be coming, too?"

"No. She . . ." Aphra began to cry. "She disappeared, too."

February 13, 433 AE, 19:30 FT, Jerusalem, Islamic State, Earth

Arliss barely made it to the transport in time. Alex was about to enter when he saw Arliss.

"Are you sure you are all right to travel, Arliss?" He walked over and hugged his friend. "I was worried about you."

Arliss noticed that Alex's eyes were void of color, but no one else seemed to notice.

"Yes. I don't want to miss this meeting."

"Okay. Please join us." He placed his hand on Mars' shoulder as they walked into the transport side by side.

The transport was long, with two rows of four seats on either side; each of those seats were filled with diplomats. They made their way into a second room with four seats on either wall that faced inward. Alex sat down next to his wife, Barbara, and Arliss sat across from him.

"I heard about the heart attack." Barbara broke the silence. "How are you doing?

"Much better, thank you. Doc says it was caused by the drastic circumstances."

"Yes. Marion told me that your son disappeared as well. He had joined that cult, hadn't he?"

"Not officially, but yes."

"Disappearances happened on Earth, too."

"Really?" Arliss had not heard that, but he was not surprised.

"Yes. The Israelis lost four-fifths of their population, dropping it from twenty million to less than four million. The Islamic State lost one tenth of its population, dropping them from nine hundred million to eight hundred ten million. The Israelis are lucky that the Islamic State's population was significantly lower than their population already. Still, the Islamic State would be much more capable of fighting the Israelis for control of Jerusalem now if it were not for the treaty, they just signed. The Israelis believed that the Islamic State was behind the events that transpired, and the Islamic State believed that the Israelis faked the disappearances in their own territories to take the blame away from them. But they did not know how widespread this event was. I told the Islamic president in order to assure him that we will back his story."

February 14, 433 AE, 11:15 FT, Jerusalem, Islamic State, Earth

Aphra walked along the marketplace and stopped in front of a vendor who sold tunics. She was drawn to one that had the patterns of a tiger on it. She gave the man the coins to pay for it and then started to look for a restroom to put it on. As she walked toward a building, she noticed a large crowd gathering at the gates of the new temple around two middle-aged men, both with medium-length black beards and long hair.

"People of Earth!" The man on the right spoke up. "Listen to our words. I am Elijah. This is my brother in Jehovah, Moses."

"You must be frightened after the events that unfolded this morning," Moses added. "But fear not, for they have left to be with Jehovah in heaven, and it is not too late to follow the true path that his Son died to create for you. All that is needed is to accept his Holy Spirit into your hearts, believe what Jesus did for you and dedicate your life to living as he would."

Aphra pushed her way through the crowd and managed to get to the front.

"He loves all of us, and that is why he has given us this chance to repent. None of us will be shorted the opportunity," Elijah continued. "If you want signs, see how Jehovah protected us from the Asiatic-Russian Alliance. The Galactic Federation was outnumbered, but the opposing ships all self-destructed. Every single one of them. That is not coincidence. Look at what Jehovah did to prove that Baal was a false God in the Old Testament."

"Look at how he helped me deliver Israel from slavery in Egypt and helped them defeat enemy after enemy in the Promised Land. There is no one greater than Jehovah."

"Stop lying to these people!" A man shot out of the crowd with a raging anger in his eyes. "This was an attack by the Islamic State, and you're trying to help them cover it up. You took my brother, and now I'll take you!"

The man aimed a gun and fired a bullet into Moses' chest. Instead of falling over, Moses stood there like nothing had happened. The wound healed rapidly, the blood disappeared and even the hole in Moses' clothing was fixed. The crowd gasped in amazement and began to talk among themselves excitedly.

"No one shall harm us under Jehovah's protection."

The man dropped his gun and pushed his way back through the crowd. That is when Aphra decided to step forward.

"How do I accept this Jehovah? Please show me." A couple of men stepped out of the crowd to join her.

Moses reached out and pulled the tunic away from her face. "This is no longer necessary.

Get on your knees and bow your head."

Aphra and the two men did so.

"Now repeat after me. Jehovah, my God, I understand that I am a sinner."

They repeated the words.

"I believe that you sent your Son, Jesus Christ, to die on the cross for our sins."

Again, they repeated the words.

"Send your Holy Spirit into our hearts and fill us with your cleansing grace."

They continued to speak the words as before.

"We now dedicate our lives to you. Show us the way to live. Amen."

After finishing the last part, Aphra opened her eyes. Moses took a flask of water from his waist and poured a little on each of their foreheads while speaking, "I baptize you now in the name of the Father, the Son, and the Holy Spirit. Rise and go to tell the nations, showing God's love to all."

Aphra and the two men split up, and as she began to head in her direction, she saw her husband standing at the door to the Embassy with a look of rage on his face. He motioned the three guards next to him to grab her, but as they moved toward her, her guard moved to intercept them. Then he realized that this was his true bosses' wishes and turned to grab her. But his momentary distraction was all she needed.

Aphra threw her tunic over his head and ran through the marketplace as quickly as she could. The guards began to close in on her. She made her way into an alley, but halfway through one of the guards caught up to her and knocked her down from behind. She turned to face him, and he threw her tunic down at her.

"Put that back on before you shame your husband any further, or I'll have orders to kill you." He pulled out a gun and was about to aim at her when he heard a clamoring behind him. Someone had rushed into the alley and knocked down the two other guards. The guard tried to turn but was also knocked out with a quick blast that came from a strange rifle. The man wore a uniform that was dark blue with light blue on the shoulders and upper chest which was lined with gold. He also wore a gold turtleneck under the uniform. His hair was short and black.

The man reached down and pulled Aphra up.

"My husband and his other guards will be close behind them."

"He sent these men after you?"

"Yes."

"Okay, then. Follow me." He led her down the alley to a strange car that was silver, long and rectangular shaped with two seats, one in the front and one in the back. She got in the back, and he jumped in the front. The engine roared to life, and the car lifted off the ground causing Aphra to feel a little disoriented. The car shot forward quickly. They stopped about eight streets over, jumped out of the car, and walked into a strange building that was very tall.

"I'll put you in protective custody while they find your husband."

"My husband is an Islamic ambassador to Israel. He has friends in high places."

He turned to her. "My friend is the prime minister of the Galactic Federation." Her eyes widened with surprise as he led her into an elevator. "I'm Arliss Mars, the chief of ministry security."

She shook his hand. "Aphra Qasim, wife of Ambassador Abdul Qasim."

CHAPTER TEN

February 14, 433 AE, 11:50 FT, Jerusalem, Islamic State, Earth

After leaving Aphra in a questioning room with two guards to protect her, Arliss made his way down the hall and snuck quietly into the negotiation room behind Alex and the newly appointed Ambassador Gail Drake. The room was like most negotiation rooms, about 150 feet long and 50 feet wide. Filling most of the room was a long table shaped like a capital "T" with a half circle at the end where Alex, Gail, and the Chief of Ministry negotiations Henrick Swancrest sat. On one side of the long table sat fifteen representatives of Israel. At the edge closest to Alex was the only one Arliss had been introduced to, Benjamin Amsel, the Israeli president. He seemed rather pleasant when Arliss was introduced to him, but now he had a look of anger on his face.

On the other side were eight representatives from the Islamic State. The closest of them was Maalik El-Fayad. He did not seem happy, either. Arliss could cut the tension in the room with a knife if he wanted to.

Finally, Alex broke the silence, "Representatives of Israel and the Islamic State, here is how negotiations with the Galactic Federation works. Each side has five minutes to state their demands. Then the other side has five minutes to make their demands. Then the three of us will deliberate in private to come up with a reasonable compromise that is fair to both parties. At the edge of each side of the table is a light. The side that lights up first will go first until the buzzer sounds. Any attempt to speak outside of your allotted time without proper procedures will result in losing all or most demands due to a penalty, unless it is determined that the side currently speaking is deliberately baiting the other side. Insults and threats are not allowed and will be dealt with in a prompt fashion." Alex pressed a blue button in front of him, and Israel's side lit up. "Israel is first. What are your demands?"

"Thank you, Prime Minister." Benjamin smiled slightly. "As you are aware, Israel has held the city of Jerusalem as a significant city to our religious beliefs, but so does the Islamic State. While our ancient temple is close to being finished with the rebuilding project you, the Galactic Federation, have started for us, we would prefer that the Islamic State choose a different city in which to build their new mosque. Their religion was formed by a false prophet that claims all non-believers should have their heads cut off. A mosque in our religious capital would be a constant reminder of the first 150 years when our people were raped, tortured, and hunted down like dogs by the more powerful Islamic State. We only recently have gained full control of Jerusalem and do not wish to lose it now. We also demand that the Islamic State no longer be allowed to reside in our city. Jerusalem is all we have left, and we are fine with that. We also need help building more apartments for housing and to expand our area to most of Arabia for purposes of growth. Also, we wish for weapons to defend our people, since the event of the disappearances has severely lowered our population. Finally, we wish for a thorough investigation into the Islamic State to find proof of their involvement in the disappearances. That is all of our demands."

Alex pressed the button, and the Islamic State's side lit up. "Okay, President El-Fayad."

"First of all, we will cooperate with any investigation that does not violate our rights as part of the Galactic Federation. Second, we wish to share fully the city of Jerusalem as equals. In fact, we wish to have all our cities on the planet rebuilt to Galactic Federation standards and have mosques in all the cities as places to worship. We will also allow the citizens of Israel to completely integrate into our society and, if they wish, build their temples in those cities as well. We wish for Jerusalem to become the capital of our planet. That is all of our demands."

"Thank you." Alex pushed the blue button and the light on the Islamic State's side of the table shut off. "We will consider all of your demands and return in two hours."

After the representatives left in an orderly fashion, Alex swung his seat around. "Arliss, how are you enjoying Jerusalem so far?"

"Enjoying it, for the most part. The food is exceptionally good, and the sights are great. I do have an issue to bring up before your meeting gets under way."

"Of course."

"I recently encountered a woman who was about to be killed by her husband for following a different religion than his. I believe under our law that would be expressly forbidden. He is an ambassador for the Islamic State here in Jerusalem."

"I see that as grounds for a justifiable divorce for her and to open an investigation of his actions. Is she here now?"

Arliss answered. "Yes."

"Then . . ."

Suddenly a large, burly man with a thick, black moustache burst into the room with a two security guards on his tail. He pointed at Arliss.

"You need to mind your own business and return my wife to me now!"

"Absolutely not. And you cannot enter this building without going through the proper channels." Arliss turned to Alex. "Shouldn't our security have stopped them before now?"

The first guard apologized. "Sorry, sir. He has twenty men with unrecognizable firearms that shoot small projectile objects that we are not equipped for. Two of our men are dead and at least three more wounded."

"I want my wife back now! I have that right under Islamic law!"

"After the treaty was signed, Islamic and Israeli law ceased to exist." Alex stood up. "You are under the Galactic Federation's law. I would study the new law well before you come barging in here. No unsanctioned weapons are allowed for non-security personnel."

"And who are you to lecture me? I'm an Islamic ambassador."

"I'm Alex Harper, prime minister of the Galactic Federation. Basically, I am your sovereign. You are violating more laws than you can comprehend right now."

"I don't care about laws given by infidels!" Abdul rushed toward Arliss and reached toward the chief of security's throat.

But Arliss side-stepped to the right and threw his left fist into Abdul's abdomen. The large man buckled over, and the two security guards tackled him to the ground and placed cuffs on him.

"You foolish thugs. None of you will leave here alive."

One of the security guards moved to the telescreen that was at the end of the room and turned it on. He switched to a camera feed in the lobby where five security guards were on their knees with their hands behind their heads and a few bodies laid on the ground near the door. Eight men stood over them with primitive guns. Twelve more stood outside the door to the conference room.

The guard spoke up. "Sir, we have the building set up for a Stun Wave. We could limit it to the hall and lobby and initiate the sound, so the personnel know to drop down."

"Do it." Alex nodded.

The guard rushed over to the security panel on the side wall and punched in some numbers. "Sir, we need two high-ranking codes to execute."

Arliss walked over to the panel and placed his hand on the screen. Alex followed him promptly. Then the security guard pressed the execute button. A second later, a loud siren rang out throughout the building. The guards on the ground quickly dropped down and before the intruders could react, a blue light passed through the hall and the lobby area. All the intruders dropped their weapons and fell to ground in a state of shock. The guards quickly stood up, and while two of the guards gathered up the weapons, the other three rushed to place cuffs on the hands of their former captors.

Back up on the hall screen, Arliss and Alex watched the guards rush out of various rooms in the hallway and cuff the remaining twelve men.

"Take them all to our makeshift prison." Arliss told the guards.

The guards escorted a confused Abdul out of the room and closed the door behind them.

Alex breathed a sigh of relief as he returned to his seat. "Well, that got the heart pumping a little. Arliss, I would like you to be a part of the discussion. Please join us at the table."

"You bet." Arliss sat next to Henrick at one of the two empty chairs on either end of the table.

"I believe we should definitely agree as a starting point that Jerusalem should be Earth's capital. I was leaning toward Islamidab, but both sides want Jerusalem to be the capital, and that's an area we can be flexible, whereas others not so much."

"I agree with that." Arliss nodded.

Henrick and Gail both chimed in with their support as well.

Alex nodded. "Good. And I am leaning toward equal rights for both sides in all the cities. Because of the conflicts with both sides, I believe we should elect a planetary governor who is from the Federation and can be impartial." After a lack of disagreement from the others, the prime minister continued. "As for the dilemma regarding religion, people everywhere are seeking a spiritual outlet because of the vanishings. I am all for letting them have an outlet, but without this god nonsense. I suggest we set up a committee to form a religious sect with moral principles taken from aspects of all religions. Henrick, could you lead that?"

"Yes, I can." The ministry negotiator nodded. "I'll form a committee to help me out."

At that time, Arliss felt called to speak up. "I think we should allow them the choice of whether or not to choose a religion that has a god involved. I see no harm in that."

Henrick spoke up. "Most of the reasons this planet has been plagued with war is due to their beliefs in fictitious gods. Without that, their reasons for hatred and animosity toward one another will die out."

"How can you say that Jehovah is fictitious after what we have all seen?" Arliss was dumbfounded. "The fact that the former prisoner, Moses, was supposed to have been executed twice and did not die is otherwise unexplainable. Plus, do you think it is a coincidence that all the enemy ships self-destructed at once?"

"He does a have a point," Gail chimed in. "Plus, the mass vanishings were mentioned word for word in the Israeli religious texts."

"Exactly. I've been studying the texts in my spare time." Arliss was enthusiastic. "Word for word, the prophecies regarding the end times are coming true. The treaty with Israel, God protecting his people from sure disaster. All of this proves that this God is real."

Alex scanned the faces of the deliberators around the table. "Well, we seem to be at a draw," he noted with a sign of dismay, "but we have a new representative that has just arrived."

The door slid open and in walked Joseph Chekov, president of the Asiatic-Russian Alliance.

"What is he doing here?" Arliss stood up defensively.

"I have signed a treaty with the Asiatic-Russian Alliance. They are now members of the Galactic Federation."

"Can we really trust them?" Gail was shocked. "Have you forgotten about all they've done? Especially when they invaded the planet Spain and destroyed most of the population."

Chekov responded, "We regret those actions deeply, and our former leader was killed in those ships that self-destructed. We implanted a virus in the ships that created the self-destruction of them all. There are a few fleets that still follow the old ways, but we are dealing with them swiftly. There is no more Asiatic-Russian Alliance. All eight of our planets will join the Federation: Ukraine, Japan, China, Philippines, Russia, Moscow, India, and Korea."

Alex spoke up. "That being said, allow me to fill you in. We agree that Jerusalem should be made the capital and that we should have a non-native to the planet be elected planetary governor. Also, that both peoples will have equal rights. But we do have a split decision regarding the global religion without a fictitious deity unless someone sways one or the other."

"Ah, yes, I remember the conversation we had last night." Chekov made his way to the end of the table opposite from Arliss.

"I move that we vote, starting with Arliss. 'Yea' is for my proposal and 'nay' is against."

After Chekov seconded the motion, the voting began.

Arliss voted "nay."

Henrick voted "yea."

Alex voted "yea."

Gail looked at Arliss, then at Chekov, and finally at Alex. She then hesitantly voted "yea." Chekov also voted "yea," making the vote four to one in favor of Alex's proposal.

Arliss was upset. He knew that having Chekov join was a power move on Alex's part. Gail had been captured by the Asiatic-Russian Alliance at one time. She had been tortured and lost two fingers and three teeth (which were later replaced). Also, her first husband had been killed in combat. She was obviously terrified.

The discussion lasted a while longer, and nothing else seemed all that bad until near the end when Chekov brought an idea to the table.

"The identification system you guys have does have some flaws. My technical experts have developed a method that has never failed in any of the tests. We tattoo a barcode on everyone's wrists or foreheads, their choice, that has a different code for each person. Security can carry portable scanners, and buildings like this can have a scanner which will not unlock the doors unless the person trying to get in has a code with the proper clearance."

"I don't believe people will be receptive of this idea." Arliss shook his head. "People here value freedom more than most, and a lot of people in the Galactic Federation will not be happy about it, either."

"I believe this is necessary. This makes it a lot easier to identify and track criminals," Alex added. "We could make it an option that those who refuse will not be able to have citizen privileges. They will not be able to buy or sell anything, vote on political matters, hold jobs, or even hold a political office. I motion that we go through with this and have a grace period of two years before the citizenship penalties take effect."

"I second," Henrick agreed.

"Okay." Alex smiled. "Let's start with Chekov."

Chekov, Gail, Alex, and Henrick all voted "yea." Arliss decided to do the same. The representatives from Israel and the Islamic State were called back in. The discussion went smoothly until Alex mentioned the godless religion.

"Absolutely not!" El-Fayad stood up and pounded the table with his fist. "There is no reason that we cannot follow Allah. He is real and will always show his wrath to those who don't follow him."

"Sit down." Alex stood up and spoke firmly, "This is no longer up for negotiation, a denial of this order will be a sign of treason."

"What about in our own homes?" asked Benjamin. "Surely that will be allowed."

"No," Alex shook his head. "Following any god will be punishable by imprisonment."

Benjamin thought for a minute. "We will follow your orders, Prime Minister."

El-Fayad sat down reluctantly.

"Who are you choosing to come in and govern our people?" asked Benjamin.

"We will provide three candidates. The first of whom will run the planet on an interim basis: Henrick Swancrest."

Arliss hid his dismay. Alex had obviously bought Henrick's vote and coerced Gail's. After the meeting, he headed back to his office and sat down to think things through.

CHAPTER ELEVEN

February 15, 433 AE, 09:36 FT, Arliss' Office,

Islamic State, Earth

Arliss sat in his office the morning after and pondered the recent events. Everything was changing too quickly. His friend was not the same person he was a few days ago. Something was very wrong. Slowly but surely, he was turning the Galactic Federation into a, dare he say, dictatorship.

Then he looked out the window and noticed a group of soldiers gathering by the front doors. They were armed in combat gear. He quickly dashed out of the office and jumped into the first elevator. As soon as he got down, he saw Henrick talking with a military commander.

"Take the two into custody for treason," Henrick told the commander.

"What is going on?" Arliss asked.

Henrick turned toward him. "Ah, Arliss, nothing to worry about, my friend. Two people are continually preaching from one of the false religions by the temple gate. They have been warned to stop but continue to persist, so we'll show our military might and nip this in the bud."

"Are you sure that's wise?" Arliss cautioned him. "We don't want a riot."

"Don't worry. The soldiers are trained to handle riots."

The commander left the building and hopped into a hovercraft. This craft was long and wide with soldiers who sat on either side. There were about twenty in all.

Arliss walked out of the building, and as they took off, he hopped onto a hover cycle and followed about twenty paces behind until they reached the crowd. The hovercraft stopped, and Arliss pulled his cycle to a stop about twenty yards behind.

"God loves all of us," Moses spoke up. "All we have to do is ask for our sins to be forgiven and let him into our hearts."

Five people came forward and went through the conversion process. Then the guards hopped out of the hovercraft and surrounded them with weapons raised.

The commander, who stood up in the craft, spoke through an announcement device that allowed his voice to be heard for a few hundred yards. "Citizens of Earth do not listen to these false teachers. They speak of impossibilities and seek to sway you from the one true religion, the only religion that is legal according to the Galactic Federation, one that has no need for a false deity. You two, known as Elijah and Moses, surrender yourselves to custody of the Federation, and you may avoid the charges of treason."

"We must remain here as our true living God demands," Elijah spoke.

"There is no one who can oppose him," Moses added.

"Guards, open fire!"

Arliss reached for his blaster and was about to draw it when the soldiers quickly fired several blasts at the two witnesses. After the blasts stopped, the two still stood there with no sign of injury at all.

Moses spoke up, "As we said, nothing opposes the will of Jehovah, the Lord God Almighty."

The surprised commander finally gathered the words. "Seize them."

The soldiers dropped their weapons to their side and started to move in.

Suddenly the area went dark as a large gray cloud moved above them. Lightning struck and took out all the soldiers. They fell to the ground dead.

"Retreat!" The commander had the driver turn the hovercraft around and race away quickly.

Arliss was about to follow when he had a sudden urge going through him.

Most of the crowd had raced away in fear. Only five people remained. An elderly couple, a civilian security guard, El-Fayad, and a young man who looked like he was homeless. They all moved over to the two preachers. The guard reluctantly looked back at Arliss. Arliss nodded at him and then hopped off his bike and joined them.

All six of them got on their hands and knees and converted right there.

As they spoke the word "Amen" in unison, Arliss felt a feeling of peace come into his body. He stood up and felt rain begin to come down heavily. He made his way back to his hover cycle and sped back to the capital, followed closely by El-Fayad. He rushed into the building as Henrick was berating the commander.

"You expect me to believe that lightning struck all your men! That is absurd! I have half a mind to find a new commander"

"Henrick." Arliss interrupted. "He is telling the truth. I saw the whole thing."

"How is that possible? They must have some sort of weapon that creates lightning."

"That's my guess," The commander told him. "We need to send a surveillance team as soon as the rain clears."

February 18, 433 AE 08:45 FT, Arliss' New Office, Jerusalem, Earth

Three days later, the rain had not stopped. That did not dissuade a crowd from gathering around the two witnesses. Arliss had switched offices, so he could see the crowd from the building. People were coming from all over to meet the witnesses, and most of them were converting. As he watched them, Moses suddenly called for silence. He and Elijah looked up at the heavens and shouted in unison.

"By the name of Jehovah, stop!"

The next thing Arliss knew, the rain had ceased, the ground was dry, and the sky was sunny and clear. Arliss was not surprised by this. He had seen too many strange things happen.

Just then, his office door slid open, and Alex walked in.

"Arliss, you ready for the . . ." He paused. "It stopped raining. It is about time; I was wondering if it would ever stop. I have never heard of instances of global rain. It must be a transitional weather phase or something."

Arliss nodded his head to fake his agreement. "Yes. I'm ready for the meeting."

"Right." Alex nodded. "See you there."

As Alex left the room, the ministerial chief continued watching the crowd. Then the door opened again and El-Fayad walked in. Arliss returned to his chair behind the desk. "What can I do for you?"

"As you know, we both converted to Christianity. I figure our true friends are going to be fewer since we hold offices that do not support the religion. Just wanted to let you know that if you ever need someone to talk to, you are not alone." He held out his hand, and Arliss stood up to shake it.

"It's good to know we aren't alone," Arliss replied.

"I found a recording of ancient Christian hymns and converted it to Federation chips. I have a bunch more that I'm hoping to smuggle back to the mainland."

"I can definitely help with that." Arliss nodded. "I will be heading back soon. Do you have one I can listen to?"

"Yes." El-Fayad produced a small chip from his pocket and handed it to Arliss. "I must be making arrangements. My assistant will meet you at your apartment tonight."

"I'll be waiting, and may Jehovah be with you."

"Always." The Islamic representative made his way out.

Arliss placed the chip in his computer. The music for the first song began to play.

"Great is thy faithfulness, great is thy faithfulness, morning by morning new mercies I see. All I have needed thy hand hath provided, great is thy faithfulness, Lord unto me."

Arliss sat there and listened to the words with a great peace coming over him. As the song finished, he noticed the time. Two minutes until the meeting. He stopped playing the music and took the chip out of the chip drive. He placed the chip in a secret pocket hidden underneath his collar and then stood up to leave for the meeting. As he rushed, Arliss remembered that he set his clock back a few minutes, so he would never be late. He slowed down as Alex came out of his office and joined him.

They made their way into the meeting room and sat down. This meeting was much smaller. El-Fayad, Benjamin, Henrick, Gail, Alex, a young man to whom Alex had not been introduced yet, and Arliss. Arliss and El-Fayad gave each other a quick nod.

Alex began. "I call the meeting to order. The first order of business is my plan to destroy all forms of the other religions. I have prepared a task force that will seek out and destroy all texts regarding Islam, Christianity, and Buddhism. Henrick, how are we doing in the establishment of a new religion?"

"I'm glad you asked." Henrick stood up and moved to the end of the room. He stood next to the telecom and started a slide presentation."

"We have an approved doctrine, which reads as follows:

> There is no God, only a set of guiding principles that we follow in our
>
> daily lives. Any text that turns us away from these principles is false
>
> and must be destroyed. The principles are to love and respect everyone

regardless of their race, age, skin color, gender, and social class. We can show love through financial support, providing homes and food for the homeless and lower class, education for those who cannot afford it, and defending against any oppressors. Showing hate toward someone is punishable by a fine or imprisonment. We shall not murder anyone; to take a life in any manner that is not self-defense is to forfeit your own life. We shall not steal; those who do owe the Federation a fine three times the worth of the stolen goods and owe the victim a fine of seven times the worth.

As Henrick went through the principles, Arliss noticed that adultery was not among them. And as the presentation ended, Alex stood up and nodded. "Well done, Henrick. When can we train teachers to preach these principles in places of learning?"

"The curriculum should be ready in two days, and we already have a list of people who want to learn."

"Excellent." Alex continued as Henrick returned to his seat and the prime minister sat down. "Now I have prepared a new security measure. The barcode I mentioned earlier will begin to be distributed tomorrow in all Federation territories. Scanners are being planted at all stores and government buildings as well as museums, schools, and train stations. There will be the two-year grace period. You cannot buy or sell anything at all but after the two-year grace period, a stricter punishment will be enforced. That punishment will be execution. I have a team that has developed a new execution device that will behead the individuals. I plan to unveil it tomorrow and have a criminal marked for death." Two guards stepped in. "That man is El-Fayad."

"What!" El-Fayad stood up as the guards grabbed him.

"Your assistant told us about your plans to smuggle Christian songs throughout the Federation. You will face execution tomorrow."

Arliss was about to stand up and object, but El-Fayad glanced at him and shook his head once. Arliss sat back in his seat and watched as the guards dragged him away.

"Won't he get a trial?" Arliss finally spoke up. "We don't want to violate his rights."

"No rights for those who commit treason," Alex reminded him. "We have to set an example."

Arliss reluctantly backed off.

"Well, that was quick and productive." Alex smiled. "Does anyone move to adjourn?"

"I move to adjourn," Gail spoke up.

Henrick seconded the motion.

"All adjourned."

February 19, 433 AE 07:17 FT, the Mars' Apartment, Jerusalem, Earth

The next morning Arliss awoke with a start and startled Marion who sat up with him.

"What's wrong?" Marion asked. "Bad dream?"

"You could say that." Arliss nodded. "What are your plans for the day?"

"Well, I plan to get the barcode."

"No." Arliss was quick to respond. "We can't get the barcode."

"But it's mandatory to buy things. I need a new dress for the party tonight."

"You can make do. We cannot take the mark."

"Why not?"

"I'll explain over breakfast."

Twenty Minutes Later

Arliss, Marion, Angela, and Paula sat around the table and finished their eggs and bacon. Arliss sipped his coffee.

Marion broke the silence. "Okay, what is this thing about the barcode?"

"Oh yeah," Angela remembered. "I figured I would get that done. I want to buy a necklace."

"No! You can't," Paula interjected, to Arliss' surprise.

"What do you mean?" Angela was confused.

"She's right," Arliss confirmed. "This barcode is the mark of the beast that was prophesied in the biblical text. I forbid anyone here to get it."

"You don't believe that do you, honey?" Marion shook her head. "There is no proof that there is an all-powerful God."

"Are you kidding me?" Arliss gasped. "You are living proof. He healed you. The doctor was completely baffled by your recovery."

"And the ships that exploded," Paula added. "I did research. There is no way a virus could infect all the ships at once. Plus, look what happened with his messengers when the soldiers tried to take them into custody. They survived several blasts from the bolt guns with no harm, and all the soldiers were struck with lightning."

Arliss added, "And you didn't see them try to execute Moses on our ship. No one could have physically survived the injection. No one."

"But it's treason to follow the religion. I've seen people who converted being arrested shortly after."

"I know times are going to be tough." Arliss nodded. "But Jehovah will watch over us, just like he did for your mother. Travis believed, and so should we. I have converted."

"So have I," Paula exclaimed confidently. "Come with me; there are some verses I want to show you." She led Angela out of the kitchen and into the bedroom.

"I guess you have a point." Marion seemed scared. "But Alex is your friend. Perhaps you can reason with him."

"I can't." Arliss told her. "He's changed. He bribed Henrick and intimidated Gale. He is the Antichrist."

Marion placed her hand on Arliss' hand.

"He was my friend, but I know now that he is lost. He accepted the Devil's deal and gained control over everything for the next seven years"

Just then a beep was heard from the front door. Arliss stood up and opened the sliding door. The man who had joined the meeting stood there. He was average height with short white hair and wore eye visors to help his sight. Two guards stood with him.

"Sir, we are inspecting all properties for religious texts. I can leave the guards outside if you are cooperative."

"Can you get back to us? We are having a family discussion, and I am chief of ministry security."

The man whispered, so the guards could not hear. "Chief Mars, I am not going to find any religious texts here except what you will allow me to copy so I can smuggle the texts back to the Federation's capital planet."

Arliss pretended to reluctantly let him in and closed the door while the guards remained on the outside.

"You're with El-Fayad."

"Yes. Thankfully, he kept our involvement to himself, so his assistant could not turn us in." "My name is Stephen Wallace. I am here on behalf of the Resistance, a movement formed by Andrew Larkendome back on Washington."

"Excellent." Arliss was relieved.

He made his way over to his desk and picked up the tablet with the biblical texts on it. He handed the tablet to Stephen who placed a chip in the chip drive and quickly uploaded all the data.

He handed the tablet back to Arliss. "We've arranged for a private ship for all followers to make their way to a safe location. You and your family can join us if you like."

"I could possibly be of help here." Arliss suggested. "But my family should go."

"If your family went missing, that would be suspicious. You would be found out too quickly. Damon Heath, your deputy chief would replace you. He is converted and part of the Resistance, but his whole family was taken in the Rapture."

"Okay then. When does the shuttle leave?"

"Next morning."

CHAPTER TWELVE

February 20, 433 AE 08:49 FT, The Mars' Apartment,

Jerusalem, Earth

Angela pouted in her room. She did not understand why her dad was being so unreasonable. She wanted to buy that dress so badly. Her father was talking with a strange young man. He was rather handsome, but she put that out of her head for now. She looked out the window of their high-rise apartment and noticed that not three feet away from her window was an escape ladder in case of a fire. She opened the window and jumped onto the ladder. She knew her athleticism would come in handy someday.

The rebellious teen quickly scaled down the ladder into the alley below. She walked out to the street and almost bumped right into Alex Harper, the prime minister and her father's good friend. Two guards grabbed her arms to pull her away.

"Angela," Alex held up his hand and the guards released her. "what are you doing here? Trying to sneak out, are we?"

"My father won't let me go shopping." She lowered her head. "And for some stupid reason, he won't let me get the barcode."

"Well, we can take care of that." He smiled. "I'll take you to one of the stations and get you rushed through the line."

Angela wondered why Alex would so blatantly go against her father's decision. Most adults would not do that, but she decided that did not matter. What mattered was buying a new necklace to show her friends.

"That would be great." Angela smiled. "For a grown up, you're not so bad."

"Well, I used to sneak out a lot as a kid. Don't tell my parents."

"Of course not."

They all stepped onto a hovercraft, and the craft started moving down the street slowly.

Around the Same Time, back in the Mars' Apartment

Back upstairs, Arliss and Stephen were busy talking about a plan to help El-Fayad escape from custody.

"I can use my position to get in and see him." Arliss suggested. "I will hand him a copy of my keycard, and he can use that to break free. We simply have to wait for him to get through the suggested back route and pick him up in a hover limo, the one that is supposedly taking me and my family to the party."

"This should work, and you visiting El-Fayad would give a perfect excuse for your hover limo being close to the building." Stephen agreed. "I will go make preparations to leave Earth. You guys should leave shortly."

Arliss nodded. "Yes." He glanced over at Marion and Paula who were listening intently from the kitchen. "Can one of you make sure Angela has her necessities packed?"

"On it." Paula made her way into Angela's bedroom and quickly came back out with a panicked look on her face.

"What is it?" Marion was concerned.

"She . . . she's gone."

Arliss rushed past her into the room. "Angela!"

He scanned the room and noticed the open window.

He rushed over to the window and looked out toward the street just in time to see Angela get into a hovercraft with Alex.

Arliss raced out of the room. "Alex has her! I'll bet anything he's taking her to get the mark."

"Hold on." Stephen cautioned. "We need to stick to the plan. I will go after her."

"You'll do everything you can to stop her?" the panicked father asked.

"Everything," Stephen assured him.

"Okay," Arliss reluctantly agreed. "He'd probably see me coming anyway."

"Well, what can we do?" Marion was terrified.

"We can pray," Paula suggested.

All four of them held hands and Paula began, "Lord, you are all powerful and all loving. Please be with Angela right now. She is in danger. Give her the wisdom to not fall for Alex's lure and get the mark. Help her get out of this dangerous situation. In Jesus' Holy Name, Amen."

"I'll leave first and then you guys shortly after." Stephen reminded them of the plan as he opened the front door.

"All clear." He moved past the guards, and they followed him down the hall.

Marion and Paula went to their rooms for a couple of minutes and returned wearing dresses. Marion's was long and black, and Paula's just barely covered the knees and was blue. They both wore dazzling jewelry and walked in high-heel glass shoes.

"You both look stunning." Arliss held both of his arms out and escorted them out of the room and into the elevator.

Five Minutes Later

Stephen had given the guards the rest of the day off and made his way down the street. He got onto his hover cycle and began to follow the hovercraft from a large distance. He rushed through an intersection as the light was close to changing red and pulled to the back of a line of crafts. There were eight crafts behind him and the prime minister.

As he sat there, he thought back to his past. Stephen had been a political student who was brought on to work with the former prime minister's campaign. His parents, who worked in the new ministry, had invited him to join them on this trip to the New Earth. He remembered the scene that frightened him nearly to death.

A Few Days Earlier

"Are you both nuts?" he yelled. "Joining this cult could be the death of your political careers—and mine!"

His father spoke kindly, "My son, you can't see what's right in front of us. There is no way this universe was designed at random. Everything was created by an intelligence. The way all the atoms and molecules work together to form everything is not done by chance."

"It's not too late, Stephen." His mother touched him on the shoulder.

"No way." He brushed her off and stormed toward the door. "You both are nuts."

As he turned toward them, suddenly, they both disappeared and left only their clothes behind.

"Mom! Dad!" He rushed over and grabbed their clothes.

He had checked for signs of radiation, thinking it was some sort of attack. But he found nothing at all. There was no other explanation for what had occurred.

Back to the Present

The ministerial hovercraft turned as the light turned green. No one noticed as a hover cycle turned shortly after them and continued to follow them. Angela watched as the craft came to a stop at the mall.

"Let's go." Alex smiled. "This won't take long."

Angela took his hand, and he helped her out onto the sidewalk. "I'm not sure about this. My father said not to."

"Well, I'm sure your father didn't mean no to this. He just does not understand completely about the implications of refusing the barcode. It is for the security of everyone in the Federation. Do not worry. This is for the best."

Angela noticed a flash of red in Alex's eyes. She realized then that something was wrong. "You know, I think I should wait for my father. You understand."

"This is not a request." Alex's smile turned to a serious frown.

Out of nowhere, a hover cycle pulled up between them. The cyclist pulled Angela on behind him and sped off before anyone could react. Two security cycles began pursuit as they sped down the main street. He turned the cycle down a small street and sped toward the road designated for hover trains. Angela held tightly around her rescuer's waist and glanced nervously as a train turned the corner and headed down the designated path. Her heart began to beat fast as they sped across the tracks just before the train sped past and blocked the two security crafts. They made a few more quick turns and ended up in an alley where they hopped off.

"Are you crazy?" Angela was still shaking. "We could have been killed."

"Better than a prison sentence for kidnapping." The man pulled off his helmet.

Then Angela recognized him. "You're the guy from before. Stephen, right?"

"That's right," he admitted. "Your father sent me. He doesn't want to leave without you."

"You're lucky I had already changed my mind about getting that mark. I think he was going to force me."

"Yeah. He probably wanted to use you as leverage to keep your father in line. Now we must hurry and change into something unrecognizable."

Stephen led her to a door. Inside was a small room which was cramped with metal shelving on either side which held metal boxes. At the end of the room was another door, and next to the door was a desk with a mirror.

He opened one drawer and pulled out two security uniforms. "This going to sound weird, but you have to remove your clothes."

He handed the uniform to her and then turned around.

"Okay." Angela quickly changed into the uniform.

He turned and placed her clothes into a metal bucket that was at the edge of the room. He grabbed a hose from under the sink and filled the bucket with a chemical that started to dissolve her clothes.

"Hey! I liked those clothes." She tried to reach in, but he pulled her back.

"It would be worse if you touched it."

He opened another drawer and pulled out a blonde wig and placed it on her head. "That will have to do."

A few minutes later and both looked completely different. They made their way out of the room and found two security cycles waiting for them. Angela looked at him curiously.

"I have good friends." He smiled and hopped onto one of the cycles. "You ever drove one of these?"

"Don't tell my father." She hopped on the other one. "He would have a fit."

She quickly turned the cycle on and raced out of the alley. After the moment of shock wore off, Stephen turned his cycle on and followed suit. Suddenly, he and Angela were surrounded by soldiers with flashing lights. One soldier made a loud announcement.

"You two are under arrest for suspicion of treason. Surrender now!"

Stephen pulled a smoke bomb out of his pocket and tossed it at the guards. He and Angela quickly drove past the guards, turned down another alley and sped out into a large highway with two hover trains headed straight for them. Stephen and Angela made it to the side of the tracks and as the train sped by, they leaped on the side. Fighting the wind, they barely made it to the back of one section and opened a door. Stephen pulled himself inside, and Angela stood there with a look of fear in her eyes. Suddenly she was terrified. Stephen reached out his hands. "Come on! I'll catch you."

Finally, Angela regained her composure. She leaped and fell. But she managed to grab onto the bars. She tried to pull herself up, but the strong force of wind pulled her down. Stephen bent down and grabbed her hands. He pulled her with all his might until she was inside. He kicked the door shut.

"We're not making the transport, are we?" Angela looked at him as she finally managed to slow her breathing down.

"I would say no. This train is heading to the opposite side of the city." He jumped up and started pressing buttons on one of the consoles. "In fact, this train is heading to Turkey. I have a few friends there, but we will have to remain in hiding. That will be harder since your wig blew away."

"What are you folks doing here?" A man in a blue worker's uniform came into the room.

"Ministerial security, sir." Stephen pointed out the uniforms as he spoke, "We hear that someone on this train is smuggling Bibles and possibly weapons. Routine inspection."

"I never heard about this. You guys have a warrant?"

"Yes. Our uniforms. Tell me, are you familiar with ministerial rules yet?"

"Not completely."

"Then get to studying. The sooner you know them, the easier of a transition this will be. Now which car has the higher-end products?"

Five minutes later

Arliss walked down the hall of the prison to the end and turned to see an empty cell. A guard passed by him, and he stopped the guard. "Where is El-Fayad?"

"In the execution hall."

"I thought it was later tonight."

"That's the beauty of technology. He's filming it now and then showing the clip at the party."

Arliss rushed into the stairwell up to the execution room. The room was surrounded by guards. El-Fayad was on his knees with his head rested on a metal slab between two metal rods. The executioner stood next to him with a black mask over his head. "I've been instructed to give you one chance to change your fate. Rebuke the God you claim to serve and hail the prime minister as your God. Your life will be spared only then."

El-Fayad stated firmly, "I will never rebuke Jehovah. He is the Almighty God."

"Very well." The executioner pressed the red button on the wall. A laser appeared across the top of the metal rods. It shot down and sliced cleanly through El-Fayad's neck. His head fell to the ground and rolled across the floor. The head stopped rolling at the feet of Arliss, who turned and walked out of the room before the guards could look in his direction. He paused for a second and collapsed against the wall.

After a minute of almost puking, the disgusted ministerial chief regained his composure and made his way down the stairs, all the way to the first floor. He walked out and saw the hover limo waiting for him. The door slid up, and he got in. As the door shut, he looked across the car at Marion and Paula.

"Where's El-Fayad?" Marion asked.

Arliss could not find the words, he sat back in the chair with a sickened look on his face. Marion knew quickly what had happened. She moved across the craft and hugged him as Paula turned on the comm and had the driver start toward the meeting place.

"I'm sorry, Sweety. I know you wanted to save him."

"It's not just his death." Arliss shook his head. "The way they killed him was barbaric. Last time I saw an execution like that, I was a prisoner of war in one of the Asiatic-Russian Alliance's concentration camps."

"I know you don't like to talk about that."

"No one should have to go through that or to be humiliated in that manner." Arliss clenched his fists. "Nobody."

Marion wrapped her arms around him, and Paula joined in on the other side.

The craft kept moving for about twenty-five minutes until it finally came to a stop and the side door slid open. They got out to find themselves in the middle of the desert. A space vessel sat down not long after. The vessel was an older model of a freight vessel that was normally used to haul products from place to place. As the back door lowered, Arliss could see that all the shelving had been removed. Two hover buses arrived. Each one carried twenty-five people.

One soldier stepped off the raft in full, black protective gear, including a helmet. The soldier took off the helmet and revealed her long, bright red hair.

"Chief Mars." She reached out her hand. "Lieutenant Brooklyn Marrows."

"Arliss, please." Arliss shook her hand. "I'm not the chief anymore."

"Of course. We don't have much time." She marched past him and motioned everyone forward.

After everyone else was on board, Arliss stood on the ramp and continued to watch for Stephen and Angela. Brooklyn joined him.

Marrows reminded him, "We have to leave. I am sure they had to hole up somewhere else. There will be more transports."

Arliss was about to turn to walk in when he noticed several large blinking lights in the distance.

"Now we have to go. They've discovered us."

Arliss realized that not just his life was on the line. He reluctantly took a step back. After the ramp closed, the vessel lifted off the ground and shot straight up into space.

CHAPTER THIRTEEN
February 22, 433AE 12:49 FT, Arliss' Office,

Orbiting Earth's Moon

Arliss sat in his new office. The resistance leader, Andrew Larkendome, obviously had a remarkably high opinion of him. After all, Andrew and Arliss had both been in the same concentration camp together. He had told the crew here that he wanted Arliss to oversee the base they were to be taken to. The last transport was on the way.

As Arliss looked out his window at the gray moon, he thought about his daughter and Stephen trapped somewhere on Earth. The thoughts of her being imprisoned under the supernatural tyrant who used to be a good friend was almost unbearable to him. Try as he might, he could not put those thoughts to the back of his head, at least not completely. He still held out hope that they had escaped and were making their way to the next transport.

Arliss stood up and put on the last piece of armor, his metallic breastplate. He made his way out of the office and onto the bridge where Captain Avery Dallas stood. Brooklyn stood at his side as his first captain. The pilot was Desmond Wells, a former soldier and, more recently, a freight pilot.

"Here they come, Captain." Desmond pointed as a small freight vessel flew around the Earth's moon and into the landing pad.

"Excellent." Dallas smiled. "Prepare the ship for departure. Let us see how many more guests we have."

The ship that Arliss was now on was a battleship that could not land on the planet due to overheating issues. This ship was four football fields long and one and a half football fields wide. Hiding behind the moon was a risk because if they used any communication systems, or powered any of their devices, the cloak would not be able to hide them from detection.

Arliss followed Dallas out of the bridge and into the elevator. The elevator started down toward the landing area, levels three through six of the eight levels.

"Looks like we are about ready to get out of here, Mars. So, you were buddies with the man himself?"

"Drew and I go way back," Arliss answered. "We were both in a concentration camp together."

"Heard you saved his life a couple of times."

"He saved mine more." Arliss tried to humble himself. "I still owe him a few."

"That's how he roped you into this."

"Didn't have to rope me in at all. This is a worthy cause that I was already trying to fight."

"No luck, huh?" Dallas pointed out.

"Not at all. Alex used to be my friend, but he sure has changed. He tried to force my daughter to take the mark to use her as leverage. Do you think she would be safe if she didn't willingly get the mark?"

"Possibly, but I can't say for sure. I only recently heard about Jehovah."

"I've heard about him over the years. But now, a lot more than before. Do we have a minister here?"

"Sure do. I will introduce you to him after we get our guests settled in. Andrew trained a team of ministers. Some have been captured and executed, but most have survived."

The elevator stopped, and they stepped off to see a crowd of people, about forty-five. They stood outside the vessel. Arliss surveyed the crowd carefully, but to his dismay, Angela and Stephen were not among them. Then he noticed they were all wrapped in blankets after coming from a heated climate on Earth.

"Did we provide those blankets?" Arliss asked.

"No," Dallas frowned.

Arliss placed his hand on the handle for his blaster.

"Sir." Desmond's voice was heard over the intercom. "Two attack vessels are approaching rapidly. Somehow they know where we are."

Dallas responded. "Take them out."

Arliss rushed to the fence overlooking the landing pad and drew his bolt gun. "Back away! It's a Trojan Horse!"

Most of the new guests threw off their blankets and started to fire, while a few guests dropped down in fear. Instantly, five soldiers were killed, but the rest took cover and started to fire back. Arliss pointed his bolt gun and started firing. His bolts killed two and injured one. Then he pulled Dallas back into the elevator while guards rushed in, continuing to fire until the few remaining attackers surrendered.

The elevator took Arliss and Dallas back to the top level, and they rushed into the bridge. The two attack vessels had just gotten into range. They were a quarter of the size of the battleship but had a lot more maneuverability.

"Raise shields!" Dallas shouted.

"Already done, sir," Desmond assured him. "Preparing for hyper speed now."

As the attacking ships started to fire laser bolts, the battleship shot into hyper speed.

"That was too close." Dallas shook his head. "We have to be more careful next time. Thankfully, this was the last stop before getting to our base."

"That could have been a lot worse." Arliss agreed. "I'm going to work on security measures. But first, they cannot be wrapped in blankets coming out, it is too easy to hide weapons. Also, they will come out one at a time. Same for entering the ship."

"I'll implement those suggestions immediately." Dallas nodded. "We cannot take any risks."

February 23, 433AE 06:05 FT, Arliss' Office, Orbiting Earth's Moon

Aphra woke up in her quarters on the battleship. She was so troubled that her parents had not reached the rebellion's launch pad in time. She remembered seeing her rescuer, Arliss Mars, among the others that made it. She looked across her quarters at her roommate. Even though the ship was large, the barracks were much smaller. The few private rooms were reserved for families and officers, so they were paired up with sleeping partners. Her partner's name was Katrina Nova. Katrina was a former prostitute with pink hair. Her hair had been dyed so many times that it stayed pink, even after she shaved it a few days ago. Now her hair was short and pink.

Aphra looked at the time clock above the door.

01:06:05:45

In translation, that was day one, Sunday; hour six, minute five, and second forty-five. There was still fifty-four minutes until they had to get up, so Aphra decided not to wake her new friend. She stood up and made her way over to the automatic drink maker. She took a good-sized, white cup from the shelf above and placed it into the device that was installed in the wall. She pressed her desired buttons, and the coffee began to pour. She loved the dark Arabian blend with some coconut milk, cashew milk, and a sugar substitute.

She made her way over to the couch and sat down. After taking a couple of sips, she picked up a tablet and logged on to the ship's mainframe to see the schedule for the day. The first item she zeroed in on was the Sunday

Service by Pastor Nathaniel Chekov. That was at 1:10:00:00, a few hours away. But prior to that, they had small group prayer meetings. All occurred in the mess hall on decks 6–7. She also noticed that at the twelfth hour was a counseling session to determine each guest's skills and figure out where they are best suited to work.

Adding all three events to her calendar, Aphra set that tablet down and picked up another tablet to read from the book of Psalms. She scrolled to a particular Psalm that she had heard about and began to read.

The Lord is my shepherd, I lack nothing,

He makes me lie down in green pastures,

He leads me beside still waters,

He refreshes my soul.

He guides me along the right paths

for His name's sake.

Even though I walk

through the darkest valley,

I will fear no evil,

for you are with me;

your rod and your staff,

they comfort me.

You prepare a table before me

in the presence of my enemies.

You anoint my head with oil;

my cup overflows.

Surely your goodness and love will follow me

all the days of my life,

and I will dwell in the house of the Lord

forever.

Aphra set the tablet down and felt a large comfort seep through her as she pondered the meaning of that passage. She knew that Jehovah would watch over and care for her no matter what. As the new convert took another sip of coffee, she heard stirring and she turned to see Katrina as the now awakened roommate sat up. Their eyes met as she jumped out of her bed and walked over to the coffee maker. She ordered a smoothie made of carrots, spinach, broccoli, tomatoes, bananas, blueberries, and mangos.

"How can you drink that?" Aphra almost cringed at the idea.

"It's healthy. Wakes you up without destroying your teeth." Katrina took her smoothie and sat down next to her. "Are you going to the service today?"

"Yeah, and the prayer meeting at oh-nine-hundred. You?"

"Yeah. I am also looking forward to seeing where I can pitch in. What is your background?"

"I am a surgeon, so definitely medical. Not sure how high up though."

"That's impressive. My skill set is not really that great except for attracting a potential husband. Are you still married to yours?"

"No. He gave me a divorce and then kicked me out." Aphra could not help but shed a few tears as she thought about that. "I tried to get him to convert, but he wouldn't have it. I don't think I'll be looking anytime soon, though."

"Me neither. I do have to admit that I am nervous. I'm not sure what I'm good at."

"Well, what other jobs have you done?"

"Really, nothing."

"Were you gentle with your clients?"

"Always. Most of them were old and disabled." Katrina shrugged.

"There you go."

"Huh?" Katrina was confused.

"Nurse. Are you organized?"

"Always. I keep all my shades of lipstick, and make-up sorted in a pattern. Jewelry, too, most of which I sold to help buy supplies for the ship."

"Good. You can keep track of medicine and all that. Come with me, and I'll tell them where to put you."

"Excellent." Katrina seemed more content.

"Until then, let's see what we can find for breakfast."

Katrina pointed at her drink.

"Okay. What can I find?"

February 23, 433 AE 06:30 FT, Arliss' Office, Orbiting Earth's Moon

Arliss woke up at the seventh hour. He glanced over at Marion, who was still asleep. He checked to make sure her alarm would still go off at eight. He stood up, made his way over to the drink maker, and placed his work mug under it. He ordered a strong, dark coffee and let the machine pour the liquid while he pulled on his uniform over his gray underclothes. He put the lid on the coffee and made his way toward the door. As he got into the hallway, he almost bumped into Captain Dallas.

"You're ready to go, ain't you?" Dallas commented.

"That's my normal workhorse mentality," Arliss admitted.

"Yeah. I am the same way. Just got up myself. Well, let us go meet the man himself."

They made their way to the elevator and rode it down to level six. They stepped off and made their way across the hall and through the sliding double doors that led into the mess hall. The hall was set up as a makeshift sanctuary with three sets of ten rows of pews. The four aisles were covered with red carpets that had been rolled out up to the stage. At the top of the stage was a large, light-brown pulpit. Behind the pulpit was a large screen that was thirty feet wide and twenty-five feet tall, almost spanning the whole two-story room.

The second level was covered up with red curtains to keep the light directed at the sanctuary. A few workers moved about setting up two crosses. The wooden symbols were on either side with a display of flowers circling around each cross. Displayed on the large screen was a picture of Jesus crucified on the cross.

Arliss stared at the display for a good minute. He knew the actual event was described as much worse, that Jesus could barely be recognizable as a human being.

He saw a man who stood at the bottom of the stairs and watched the workers make the finishing touches. The man turned and looked at the two newcomers and headed toward them.

"Captain Dallas." He shook the captain's hand firmly.

"Pastor Chekov," Dallas greeted him. "This is Arliss Mars. He will be leading the new base on Planet Argentina."

"Pastor Chekov." Arliss reached out his hand.

"Nathaniel, please." Nathaniel shook Arliss' hand. "Good to meet you. I hear your son is one of the departed."

"Yeah. It gave me a heart attack."

"I lost my daughter, but I wasn't there when it happened. I was actually yelling at the guy who converted her when he disappeared."

"That had to be a wakeup call." Arliss remarked. "My wife and daughter aren't converted yet, and my daughter did not make it aboard. My adopted daughter, Paula, is now converted."

Nathaniel responded, "Sorry to hear about your daughter. Our prayers are with her. That is good. The former prime minister's daughter, correct?"

"Yes. Jack and I were good friends, and so were she and Angela. I'm curious, what does the scripture say about infidelity?"

"As I understand it, the scripture says that we shall not commit adultery. In fact, that was so high a sin that it made it to the Ten Commandments that God gave Moses originally. I'll be starting a series on that as soon as we make it to the base."

"I look forward to that," Arliss nodded. "I heard there are some prayer meetings in about an hour."

"Yes." Dallas announced. "Say, why don't the three of us grab breakfast and then meet down here for that?"

"Sounds like a plan," Nathaniel agreed.

Three days after Jesus' Death

Four Roman guards stood outside the tomb, each with a spear in one of their hands. Over the mouth of the tomb, a large boulder had been rolled to block all entry. Night had fallen, and stars were starting to appear in the sky.

"I don't understand why Pilate wants us to guard this tomb." The first guard shook his head.

"We should not complain about our orders." The second shook his head. "You don't want the captain to hear you. That will be another day's rations."

"I still don't get it though. Who would steal the body of a Jew? They are scum who are ungrateful for the Romans who protect them. If you ask me, the whole lot of them should be wiped out."

"Careful," The third guard warned. "The captain has a soft spot for Jews. Particularly this one. He healed the captain's servant."

As the third guard finished speaking, a light appeared above the tomb. The four guards turned and raised their spears up toward the light. In the center of the light stood what looked like a giant man, at least twelve feet tall. He carried a large sword in his hand and stared down at them with fiery eyes.

The guards collapsed onto the ground and fell asleep.

The angel jumped down and rolled the large boulder aside. The angel stepped back and waited until Jesus walked out of the tomb. He wore a white robe and glowed brighter than the angel. The angel disappeared, and Jesus walked past the guards and into the garden nearby.

The Following Morning

Mary Magdalene and Martha made their way down to the tomb.

"Do you suppose the guards will let us in to pour the perfume on Jesus' body?" Mary asked.

"God willing." Martha crossed her fingers. "Joseph has some sway with them since he paid for the tomb. I hope we don't have to get him to come and act on our behalf."

They reached the tomb and saw that it was open. The guards were sleeping on the ground where they were supposed to be standing.

They rushed to the tomb as tears came down their faces, and they both fell to the ground.

"Who would do this?" Mary started to shake with anger.

Just then a man appeared at the doorway in front of them.

"Why are you both crying?"

After a moment of shock, Mary spoke up. "They have taken my Lord away. I do not know where they have put him. Do you, Gardener?"

"Mary." The man spoke to her.

She looked up at him and her tears became tears of joy. "Teacher."

Jesus replied, "Do not hold on to me, for I have not yet ascended to the Father. Go instead to my brothers and tell them that I am ascending to my Father and your Father, to my God and your God."

"Yes, Lord." Mary and Martha stood up and rushed away.

CHAPTER FOURTEEN
February 23, 433 AE 09:30 FT, Secret Location

The room was dark and cold. Twelve hooded figures gathered around the long table and waited. A couple of them started to grow restless. One glanced around the room and kept tapping his fingers on the table. Another kept looking back at the door. Finally, the first one stopped tapping his fingers and broke the silence.

"Is he going to arrive anytime soon? He's never had a problem with punctuality before."

"To be fair, this is last minute." The one next to him spoke up. "He's never steered us wrong before."

Then the door opened, and a thirteenth hooded figure emerged and sat at the table as the door slid shut behind him.

"As all of you know, we have a serious problem with the disappearances. Many are turning to faith despite our new minister's plan to make faith in a God other than him illegal. Personally, I think he went overboard in saying that we should worship him as a God, but I still think he is our best chance at erasing religion for good. We need to get close to him. Have an aide whisper in his ear and manipulate him into being an advocate for our plans. What are your thoughts?"

"I am with you." The hooded figure next to him spoke. "We must get him in our pockets like we had Priest."

"Do you really think it's wrong to worship him as a god, though? He could get angry if he finds out that we don't."

All heads turned to one figure in the back.

"Who are you that speaks? You are in Martin's position, but you do not sound like him."

"Well, if you have to ask . . ." The figure stood up and removed the hood.

Everyone stood up in shock for he was Prime Minister Alex Harper.

"Mr. Harper. How did you find out about us before we approached you?"

"Oh, not to worry. Martin was a friend of mine—*was* being the key word. You see while I do believe science is important, I believe that religion is necessary. And I certainly am not a puppet for any secret organization. Well, at least not yours. And I must say that I cannot tolerate any interference from you gentlemen."

Alex's eyes became red, and the room started to heat up rapidly. The men tore off their robes, including the one at the head of table. The Patriarch fell back into his chair and wiped sweat off his brow.

"What is going on here?" The Patriarch was scared.

"Oh, it's quite simple." Alex walked across the room with no sweat coming from his body, and he sat on the table near him. "Instead of sending you all to hell, I'm bringing hell to you. Then he stood up and raised his hands wide. All twelve men floated up in the air. Their skin began to develop large blisters, and then they began to burst into flames until nothing was left of them except for ashes. The room then turned to normal temperature.

The door slid open, and a young man rushed in. "What is going on here?"

The man then noticed that he was in the presence of the prime minister. He fell to his knee and bowed his head.

"I was simply seeing if this room was suitable for use. Not yet. Do get this place cleaned out. Maybe I'll use it for more storage."

"Of course, Your Holiness."

Alex walked out of the room, whistling a cheerful tune.

February 23, 433 AE 09:35 FT, Fort Wells, near the City of Dallas on the planet, Texas

General Potter sat in his office with tension in his heart. He did not like the alliance with the Asiatic-Russian Alliance. They were bad news and always had been. The door to his office slid open, and in walked Commander Hayfield of the GF Naval Fleet.

"Commander Hayfield." The general stood up and shook his hand. "What is a naval officer doing at an army base?"

"Well, sir, I'm here to see you." Hayfield sat down, as did the general. "You see, I know that you dislike the way the prime minister is running things. So do I and a bunch of others high up in the military. We need to do something to stop him, and we believe that you are the right man to lead us."

"Who is we?" The general was curious.

"Eight Naval fleets and over two-thirds of the ground forces in the Army and the Marine Corp."

"What do you have in mind?" The General was afraid to ask.

"We take Washington."

"Washington. That would be impossible."

"Not if six of their ten fleets are part of the eight fleets I mentioned before. Plus, we have spies in all the other fleets that have set up a way to sabotage the remaining fleets' weapons systems. This will be the easiest takeover we have seen. Local security will not be enough to stop us."

General Potter glanced out his window and thought for a moment. The plan was a particularly good one. The prime minister would be unwilling to allow harm to come to his precious capital by risking taking the city back by force. He stood up.

"I'm in. When do we leave?"

Hayfield stood up and shook his hand. "In two hours."

February 23, 433 AE 09:58 FT, The Battleship

Arliss made his way into the sanctuary and sat near the front as everyone else gathered in. Pastor Chekov walked up the stairs to the podium and turned to face everyone.

"Greetings everyone. Thank you all for attending. My name is Nathaniel Chekov. I was an ambassador for the Asiatic-Russian Alliance, formerly stationed in Washington. Like all of you, I was stunned when our loved ones, friends, allies, and even some enemies disappeared, some right in front of us. I did not study the Bible as an occupation and only recently started reading from this book after my daughter disappeared. Like all of you, I wanted to know more. The prime minister has tried to explain this away through a theory that there was a weapon of some sort that was created by terrorists within the Children of Jehovah. As hateful as I was toward them, even I knew better than that. They never lifted a hand against us, not even to defend themselves. In a world that has been overflowing with sin and darkness, they showed us mercy—a mercy that we do not deserve.

"Romans 3:23 says, 'For all have sinned and fall short of the glory of God.' That means that not one of us is perfect, contrary to what some of us have thought. I had those moments. I lived in a mansion and had servants waiting on me hand and foot. But was I perfect? Absolutely not. I fell to the sin of greed. I stole money from my government countless times to support my luxurious living. But there is hope for me, and there is hope for all of you.

"Romans 6:23 says, 'For the wages of sin is death, but the gift of God is eternal life through Christ Jesus our Lord.' And John 3:16 says, 'For God so loved the world that He gave His only Son, that whoever believes in Him shall not perish, but have everlasting life.' God sent his own son to die on the cross and pay the price for our sins. Not only did he die on the cross, but he was beaten and whipped until he was not recognizable as a human being. His flesh was torn. His blood was spilled. His life was taken. All that done so that we could be forgiven of our sins and would be able to enter into an eternity with him in heaven. All we have to do is believe what he did for us, invite him into our hearts and promise to live our lives as his ambassadors to the world. If anyone of you feels it in his heart, I ask you to come forward during our time of singing and go through the prayer with one of the staff members who are standing against the far walls.

"Father, I thank you so much for giving us this precious gift. For giving us another chance to repent of our sins and join you in heaven. As we enter these troubling times, I pray that you give us hope, strength, peace, wisdom, and patience so that we can truly be your ambassadors to the world. I pray for our leaders so that you give them the proper discernment when making decisions for us, and I also pray for our enemies. I pray that you soften their hearts and help them come to know you so that they too can be washed clean of their sins. In Your holy, righteous name. Amen."

As he finished, music began to play and the words to a hymn began to play as several people left their seats and made their way to the side walls.

Great is thy faithfulness, oh God my Father,

There is no shadow of turning with thee,

Thou changest not, thy compassions they fail not,

As Thou hast been Thou forever wilt be.

Great is Thy faithfulness, great is Thy faithfulness,

Morning by morning, new mercies I see,

All I have needed Thy hand hath provided,

Great is Thy faithfulness, Lord unto me.

After a few more hymns everyone had returned to their seats, and Josiah returned to the podium.

"This evening, at the sixteenth hour, I will hold a class for the new believers, so we can learn about how to live a life according to God's will and be a light to those around us. I thank all of you for coming and God bless you."

February 23, 433 AE 12:13 FT, The Battleship

Aphra sat in the interview station and waited for the interviewer to return to the room. Her thoughts went to her parents, who were still stuck on Earth. She worried for their safety and even more so about their faith even if her reunion with them would have to wait until the millennial kingdom. She hoped they would not recognize Alex Harper as their god. Her father was a stubborn man, so he would not be so easily intimidated by the prime minister and his ambassadors.

Finally, after a few minutes of waiting, the staff member returned.

"Sorry about the wait, Aphra," he apologized. "There were a lot of hold ups in the line. We do have need of you in the medical bay. In fact, you are the most qualified to be chief medical officer, temporarily here and then permanently at the home base. I assume that would be satisfactory."

"Yes. That's better than I thought." Aphra was stunned. "I also wanted to speak on my roommate's behalf. Her former occupation was prostitution. I think she would make a great nurse. Her name is Katrina Nova."

"Of course. I will investigate that. As for compensation, we do not exactly have a perfect situation right now. Once we get to the base there will be better quarters for the higher staff, but as far as the rest goes, meals will be provided and at least two thirty-minute breaks a day if the time can be afforded."

"Of course. That will be fine."

"Good. You are to report to the medical bay at 02:06:00:00 tomorrow. We do not have many wounded right now, but health inspections are required for all personnel, day three through day six. We will be scheduling the appointments for all personnel throughout the day."

"You got it." Aphra stood up and shook his hand. "Will I have anyone to assist me?"

"Yes. We already have a few nurses scheduled to start. Medical Bay will be open twenty-four hours a day, and each set of nurses will be on 12-hour rotations. You will have an administrator, but that position has not been filled yet."

"Very well. I look forward to meeting him or her."

Aphra made her way out and ran straight into a young man. His coffee spilled all over her, and they paused in a moment of embarrassment.

"I am so sorry, miss." He ran and grabbed some paper towels to help wipe the coffee off her shirt. "I really need to learn to be more careful. Good thing I like iced coffee."

"It's okay." Aphra took the paper towels. "Thankfully, I don't have any plans tonight."

"Well, that's a relief."

"After all, I think it was my fault. Let me buy you a new cup of coffee."

"The coffee is free," he smiled, "but you could allow me to treat you to dinner."

"Really? You just met me."

"I probably don't know anyone here. So, this is a start. I am Phillip. You are?"

"Aphra. Okay, sure. Maybe meet me here at the eighteenth hour."

"You got it. Well, I have got to run. Hopefully, I will be placed, too, by that time."

She watched him go into the interview room. Phillip was handsome. Then she wondered, even though her husband had given her a divorce, was she still bound to him in the eyes of God? She decided that she should find the pastor and ask his advice.

At that moment, a loud blast occurred, and as Aphra was thrown over a desk, everything went black.

At the Same Time, Arliss' Office

Arliss sat in his office and took the last bite of the salad he had ordered for lunch. As he munched on the crisp lettuce, he looked at his pad at the file for the man who would be the deputy chief of security. The man would be here in a few minutes. He finished the bite and then set his plate and silverware to the side. His assistant, Gloria, walked in.

"Sir, a Mr. Braukendom is here to see you."

"Yes. Send him in."

"And I'll take that for you."

Gloria stepped forward and grabbed the plate and silverware off the desk. She exited quickly, and a tall man, appearing to be in his early thirties, walked in.

"Mr. Braukendom." Arliss stood up and held out his hand. "It's good to meet a fellow Washingtonian."

"Good to meet you, too, sir." The new deputy chief shook hands with his new boss. "And please, call me Phillip."

"Very well, Phillip. Have a seat."

They both sat down on either side of the desk, and Arliss took a sip of his coffee.

"So, I see you went to Pittsburgh University." Arliss noted.

"Yes, sir. Top of my class."

"That's great. Same here. Well, second to top. Who did you learn under?"

"Alistair Worthingly."

"He's still teaching there?"

"Not anymore. He vanished with the others."

"Well, that's good to know. You have quite a stellar record; I can see why they picked you for the job. You saved yet?"

"Yes, sir. I was saved a few days before . . ."

A loud blast was heard, and the room shook. They both stood up and rushed out the door, following a group of guards that were running toward the docking bay with all the interview stations. They made their way out to the deck and looked out see a blast hole with a radius of eighty feet. Around the hole was a lot of debris, and people everywhere were either hurt or dead. Most were covered in blood.

"Close off the area to all non-emergency personnel!" Arliss shouted and then turned to Phillip, "I want to know the source as soon as possible. Get the investigation team in, pronto."

"You got it." Phillip got onto the comm system and started barking orders as they both took the elevator down. As the investigation team made their way to the blast site, he noticed Aphra lying behind a desk near the elevator and rushed over to her. He opened her eyes and quickly called an EMT team over.

"This one has a concussion."

"Understood." The lead EMT nodded and carefully lifted her onto the hover stretcher and hauled her out.

"You know her?" asked Arliss.

"Just met her today. Asked her on a date."

"I met her back on Earth, such a shame."

"I think she'll pull through though."

February 23, 433 AE 14:32 FT, The Battleship

Aphra woke up with a start and sat up. She glanced around to see all the other people lying in hospital beds around her. She saw a pad nearby and picked it up. The pad showed her chart, documenting that she had a concussion. That would explain the headache. But she had no broken bones or muscles and only a few scrapes. She stood up.

"Miss." A nurse ran up to her. "You need to remain in bed. We're trying to locate the doctor right now."

"I am the doctor."

"Oh. Um, you have a . . ."

"Concussion. I know. I am still the best shot we have of saving people. Give me the list."

"List?"

"The list of people that need to be treated."

"We haven't gotten that far yet."

"Then start. In order of most importance. Who needs surgery or treatment now? Who can wait?"

"Okay." The nurse grabbed a pad and started to review the files. "The patient across the hall has a limb that is half off. We've been trying to stop the bleeding."

Aphra rushed across the hall and saw a couple of nurses trying to hold a young woman's leg together and use clothes to stop the blood. She ran over and pushed the nurse on the right to the side. She took one glance at the leg and knew what had to be done.

"Laser blade."

The nurse found a small metal device and handed the object to her. Aphra turned it on, and a red laser protracted from the device about six inches.

"Hold her steady."

"No!" The woman cried. "Not my leg. Just fix it."

"I'm sorry." Aphra looked the woman in the eye. "But that is not possible. You will be a lot worse off if I do not amputate. Do you give me permission?"

The woman thought for a moment and then nodded. The nurses held her still, and Aphra guided the laser and sliced through the small bit of skin and flesh that held the leg together. The lower leg fell onto the bed and Aphra turned off the laser, set it down, and picked up a large syringe. She placed the syringe at the bottom of the upper leg and injected a foam onto the open wound which quickly began to seal as the foam became a skin-like substance and stopped the bleeding. She set the syringe down and then looked around the room. No other patients were in bad shape, so she headed back out where the first nurse was still going over the list.

"Who's next?"

February 23, 433 AE 20:51 FT, The Battleship

Aphra had finally gotten done making her rounds with all the patients, and she sat down in her office for a break.

The first nurse, who Aphra learned was named Kathrine, walked in.

"Yes, Kathrine."

"Chief Mars wants you to sign off on all the deceased and also commends you on a good job."

"Okay. Tell him thanks."

Aphra stood up and stretched her arms. Then she grabbed her pad and walked out of her office. Thankfully, the morgue was right across the hall from her office. She stepped in and unzipped the first bag to reveal an elderly man. She found his file in the pad and signed it. Seventeen others were deceased. Finally, she came to the last black bag. She unzipped the bag and as soon as she looked at the head, her heart sank. She set the pad down, half-sat on the gurney, and cried as she looked down at Katrina Nova.

CHAPTER FIFTEEN
February 24, 433 AE 06:45 FT, The Battleship

Aphra sat in the mess hall and stared at her breakfast. Her grief was extraordinarily strong at the moment. She could tell that Katrina and she would have been great friends. She picked up the container of sugar and started pouring the stuff into her coffee, not really paying attention to the amount.

"You going to have some coffee with your sugar?"

"Huh?" Aphra looked up to see Phillip standing there with a tray of food in his hand.

Then Aphra realized she was continuously pouring a ton of sugar into her coffee and suddenly stopped.

"You obviously had your mind elsewhere."

"Yeah. I lost a good friend in the explosion."

"Oh, yeah. Mind if I sit down?"

"Go ahead."

Phillip sat down across from her. "Sorry to hear about your friend. That is tough. You think you will be able to make it?"

"I hope so. I am the chief medical officer now, so I must. Besides, she was saved at the service earlier. I saw her go up."

"Then she's in a better place with Jesus. It is said that there is a special place for martyrs. They may even become part of God's army for the final battle."

Aphra nodded. Other things were on her mind as well. "I'm also worried about my parents. They did not make it onto the ship or any other, for that matter. What job did you get?"

"I am the deputy security chief," Phillip told her.

"Oh, so you know Arliss Mars?"

"Yeah. He is my boss."

"I have a meeting today with the other chiefs. Why don't we meet up after that?"

Aphra could not believe that she said that.

"You bet. I still owe you a date anyway. What are your parents' names?"

"Aaqil and Dariyah Khaleel."

"Khaleel, that's a nice last name. So Aphra Khaleel, you want to be here at the eighteenth hour for dinner?"

"Yes, but it's Qasim for my last name. My ex-husband gave me a divorce, but I did not have time to change my last name back."

"A divorce?" Phillip was concerned.

"Yes. When he learned that I converted, he wanted nothing to do with me."

"Oh, I see. Well, I am looking forward to the dinner."

"Me, too."

"Okay then. I'll see you then."

He took a bite from his eggs benedict.

February 24, 433 AE 07:02 FT, A Battleship Orbiting Washington

Commander Peter Matthews sat in his office in the battleship Lincoln. He stared down at the beautiful planet he had sworn to defend. Washington had a land mass that made up about three-tenths of the entire planet. The rest was made up of water. Washington was three times the size of the ancestral Earth. Thankfully, an invention called the graviton stabilizers sets up fields around cities and most areas around the planet to make the gravity similar to Earth's allowing humans and other creatures to survive.

He remembered growing up on a large farm and learning the craft. His father had been disappointed at his choice to join the Galactic Federation Military. But finally, he saw that his son only wanted to ensure that their planet was safe.

An alert began to sound, and he rushed out onto the deck.

"Captain on the bridge!" came a shout near the door.

"Report!" He made his way to his chair and sat down.

His security officer spoke up. "Sir, an unscheduled arrival of military vessels has appeared."

"Our military?"

"Yes, sir. Two fleets."

"Hail them."

The communications officer hailed them, and one of the two ships' bridges appeared on the screen with General Potter standing front and center.

"General Potter. This is an unexpected surprise. What can I do for you?"

"You can stand your ships down, Commander. We are taking Washington."

"What do you mean taking Washington?"

"I represent a group that does not like the way our prime minister is running things. We are taking his capital and will return it once he chooses to resign."

"Absolutely not. You are outnumbered, General."

"Sir," The security officer interrupted, "six of our own fleets have surrounded us and are aiming their weapons directly toward us."

"I'm not as outnumbered as you think. It's best for the sake of the civilians that you back down."

"I will not surrender."

Suddenly the engineering officer pulled out a bolt rifle and aimed it at the security officer. The deputy commander came into the room with ten armed guards as the communications officer stood up and aimed another weapon at the commander.

"I was afraid you would say that. Thankfully, I know you and planned for that exact response." General Potter smiled. "Are you willing to surrender now?"

The enraged commander reluctantly nodded. "You all will be court martialed for this."

February 24, 433 AE 08:45 FT, Alex Harper's Office, Jerusalem, Earth

Alex Harper sat in his office, humming a joyful tune. Everything was going according to plan, except for the few rebels, but they would be taken care of soon enough. He scrolled through the morning report, and seeing no sign of trouble, he leaned back and took a sip from his glass of wine.

The front door slid open, and his young assistant walked in with an incredibly nervous look on her face. He knew quickly that something bad had happened and stood up. "What is it, Allison?"

"Sir, a militia has taken over Washington. They are demanding that you resign, or they will destroy the planet."

"What?!"

Alex pounded his fist on the table, and Allison gave a start. Alex then tried to calm himself so that he could think rationally. "Who is claiming leadership of the group?"

"General Potter."

"He's bluffing."

"Are you sure?"

Alex remembered that Allison was from Washington. "Yes. I am positive. I know him. I did not see this coming, but I know he will not pull that trigger when it comes to it." He turned on the telecom and Commander Smith appeared on the screen.

"Your Holiness. I assume you've heard about the situation on Washington."

"Yes. I am positive Potter is bluffing. How many fleets do we have within range?"

"Four, sir."

"Do you trust their commanders?"

"Absolutely."

"Good. Send them to the planet Texas and leave no one alive."

"Sir. Are you . . ."?

"Yes!" He paused. "Yes. I am sure. Potter will have no choice but to leave and defend his home planet. His family is there."

"Yes, Your Holiness."

The screen went blank.

"Do you need anything else, Your Holiness?" Allison asked.

"No. You can return to your duties."

"Yes, Your Holiness." She hustled her way out of the room.

"General Potter won't know what hit him."

February 24, 433 AE 12:45 FT, *The Battleship*

Aphra made her way into the conference room. At the head of the table was a telecom with Andrew Larkendome visible. Sitting on the far end of the right side of the table was Arliss Mars. A door right behind him led directly into his office. Next to him sat Commander Dallas. Next to him was Chief of Human Resources Ellen Rockwell. Across from Ellen sat e Communications Officer David Millstone, and next to him was Chief of Engineering Phil Marksmith. The seat next to Phil was empty. Aphra made her way down the table and sat down.

"Hello, everyone," Andrew spoke up, "I wish I could be here with you all. But I am preparing the base. First order of business: we had to change the location to Arctican, the ice planet. The next closest planet is Texas. For some reason Texas' fleets have been called away, so now is the best time to pass that planet."

"If I may ask, do you know the reason Texas' fleets were called away?" Arliss interrupted. "I find that very suspicious."

"Yes. They are part of a different resistance force that has just taken Washington."

"Taken Washington?" Arliss was concerned.

"Peacefully. But they have threatened to destroy the planet if Alex Harper does not resign. I believe that General Potter is bluffing, however. The problem is that I believe our prime minister will see through that, too. He is evil, but he is not dumb. How are things on board?"

"We had an explosion on one of the decks. Thirty dead. A few injured critically and forty with minor scrapes, bruises, and concussions," Aphra told them. "We will be needing a prosthetic leg for one woman and two prosthetic arms, one for large man and one for a small child."

"We have the machines to design such equipment." Andrew assured her. "Have you discovered who planted the bomb and how?"

"It was a suicide bombing." Arliss told him. "We are working to discover if the terrorist had any allies."

"Very well. I am hoping you find them before you arrive. We have an intense screening setup, just in case."

"That's good." Arliss nodded. "Chief Engineer, report."

Phil spoke up, "Everything is fine so far. We found a couple of glitches in the system, but nothing out of the ordinary."

"Great. Chief of HR, report."

"We only have twelve people who do not have positions at this time. They are undergoing training, however. Two want to be nurses. Eight want to be security, and two want to be cooks. We have also started a schooling system for the young children focusing on positions that may be available when they grow up and also religious curriculum."

"That's good to hear. Communications Officer, report."

David responded, "We noticed a small signal that may be coming from a spy."

"When did you find that?" Arliss was caught unaware.

"Just before I came in here. I suggest we wait until we find the source and eliminate it."

"I agree. Even with the opening clear, we cannot lead the enemy directly to our doorstep," Arliss spoke up.

"Yes. This is overly concerning."

"I already have men trying to locate the signal. We have it narrowed down to this deck."

"I will have all the offices searched." Arliss stood up. "If that is all . . ."

"Yes." Andrew nodded. "I will let you get to your manhunt."

February 24, 433 AE 14:45 FT, The Battleship

Aphra walked down the hall toward Phillip's office. The door was partly open, and she overheard a mechanical voice speaking.

"Thank you for giving us the location of the new base. We will send a fleet there as soon as one comes available."

"Just follow my orders. I need to lay low for the time being. They discovered the signal." Phillip responded. "For His Holiness."

"For His Holiness."

Phillip turned to see Aphra in the doorway. She turned to run as he raced after her. No one else was in the hall.

"Come back! Aphra, you misunderstood."

She made her way to a weapons locker and pulled out a blast pistol. She aimed the weapon at him, and he stopped and held up his hands.

"Aphra. It is not what you think. Allow me to explain."

"Explain what? You're a spy."

"No. I was faking. Just give me the weapon."

"Faking?"

"Yes. We found the real spy, and I managed to pretend to be him and give them a false location. You trust me, right?" He held out his hand. "Just give me the pistol."

"I want to believe you, but I can't take any chances. Call Arliss here on your comm device."

He knocked the gun out of her hand and grabbed her. He dragged her into a nearby closet as she tried to fight him. He threw her to the ground and was about to punch her when she kicked him in the groin. As he was stunned, she got up, grabbed a garbage can and threw it at him. He fell to the ground as she raced back into the hall. She saw two security guards walking toward her.

"Help!" They rushed over to her.

"What seems to be the problem, miss?" Asked the first officer. She turned to see Phillip rush out of the closet and pointed at him. "He's the spy!"

He pulled his blast pistol and shot at them but missed. Then he turned and ran around a corner, out of sight, as the two guards followed in pursuit.

February 24, 433 AE 15:13 FT, The Battleship

Aphra sat in the security office and sipped a cup of tea. She could not believe that she had trusted Phillip. How could she be so wrong about someone? Could her judgment be that off?

She looked up to see Arliss come out of his office. He sat next to her.

"Don't be too hard on yourself. I trusted him, too. He seemed like an honest guy, but he was simply really good at his job."

"What will happen to him?"

"We will hold a trial for him at the base and decide his fate there."

"I guess I wasn't looking for signs of distrust. I was caught up with the death of my roommate."

"Sorry to hear that. I have lost quite a few friends in my years in security. It stays with you. The best we can do is move on and live our lives like they would want."

"Yeah. Besides, I know she is with Jehovah in Heaven. I should get to the medical bay and get checked out. Thank you for the talk."

"Anytime."

CHAPTER SIXTEEN

February 24, 433 AE 15:30 FT, City of San Antonio,

Planet Texas

San Antonio was blooming with life as people hustled around, going to shopping malls, visiting cafes, and playing sports. One man was jogging along a walkway that crossed an artificial body of water. He was the first to see it. A large fleet of the oval-shaped attack crafts entering the atmosphere. "Must be a drill," he thought as he watched them come in. But then a laser shot from the lead craft completely obliterated a nearby cafe.

The other ships began to fire as people began to panic and run anywhere they could, but there was nowhere to hide. The man turned to see a hover train station blow up and take four trains and several loading decks with it. They took out all the train stations methodically, then the large shopping malls and large towers. No one could hide, and no one was safe. The death toll was already in the triple thousands and getting higher.

February 25, 433 AE 06:45 FT, Potter's Battleship in Washington's Orbit

Potter stood in his new office on his battleship, the *Daniel Boone*. He was incredibly pleased with his moves. He had received no word from the Galactic Federation, but he knew that they would not risk losing their precious capital planet.

The doors to his office slid open, and the communications officer came in with a very frightened look on his face.

"What is it?"

"Sir. The Galactic Federation has attacked and wiped-out Texas."

"What?" The general sunk down into his chair. "The whole planet?"

"Y-yes, sir. The report is that close to thirty million people are dead."

Potter glanced at the picture of his wife and three children. He lowered his head and began to cry as the communications chief stood there in awkward silence.

"Would you like a handkerchief, sir?"

"Get out."

"I beg your pardon?"

"Get out!"

The general jumped up and threw a paper weight at the officer. The poor man managed to duck and then raced out of the room. As he shook in a mixed flurry of anger and sadness, Potter made his way over to the window and looked down at the capital city.

"I know what you are thinking."

The general turned to see his new colleague, Commander Hayfield, who stood at the doorway.

"No one could have ever predicted how evil Prime Minister Harper could be. He actually claims to be a deity."

"Obviously a soulless one."

"Destroying Washington will only prove that he was in the right. I think most people here would side against him if we let them know what is going on. We've collected video footage of the attacks."

"No survivors."

"Sorry. We searched but came up with nothing. Also, he wants you to make a mistake and go after him in a fit of rage. That cannot happen."

Potter reluctantly nodded. "I also want to get my hands on the scumbags who actually decided to go through with the order. I mean really, who in their right mind would do such a thing? I would take treason over that. Let us tell Commander Matthews. I think he would side with us once hearing about this. He had a sister in Albuquerque."

"I am preparing to tell him everything now. Do you want the honors?"

"I need time. You should tell him."

"Very well, sir. Are you going to be, okay?"

"No, but I'll muster through it."

"Okay."

Hayfield left the room, and Potter quickly reached into his desk and pulled out his bolt pistol. He sat down and continued to weep for his family. He could not believe they were gone, along with his friends.

February 25, 433 AE 07:15 FT, The Battleship

Matthews sat in the interrogation room with a horrified look on his face as he watched footage of Albuquerque being destroyed. Hayfield stood next to the telecom.

"They took out the entire planet?"

"Population close to eight hundred million dead."

Matthews shook his head and stared at the table, not wanting to see the scene unfold anymore. He was trained to tell when a video was fake, and there was no way that was fake.

"I can you give you some time to . . ."

"What do you want me to do?"

"Are you going to join our cause?"

"You can bet every bit of currency you have. I'm all in."

"I figured you would say that. We want you to take a fleet and find any other fleets in the region. Show them what happened and see what they think. If they side with Harper, wipe them out. We have a new defense and weapons system that will make the normal fleets almost useless."

"You got it."

"Great. We will have you command the *NO Liberation*. NO stands for New Order."

"When do we leave?"

"Tomorrow morning. Preparations are being made as we speak."

February 25, 433 AE 08:45 FT, Bridge, Battleship

Arliss stood by Commander Dallas as they traveled past the planet of Texas. He looked at the massive planet in awe. Texas was twice as large as Washington and had the largest population in the galaxy. He wondered why the large planet was left unguarded. He knew Potter would never do that without good reason. Was taking Washington really that important?

Arliss noticed that most of planet had fiery red light glowing from it. Then he realized.

"Commander, look!"

"Huh?" Dallas was confused.

"Those glowing lights. That's not light. That's fire. It's all over the surface."

"Comm officer, can you zoom in?" Dallas asked.

"Yes, sir."

The comm officer zoomed the screen past the layers of atmosphere, and they all gasped in horror. Not a place on the planet was left untouched. Every bit of land was blackened, and not one building in any city was left standing. The entire planet was in ruins.

"How could this happen?" Arliss shook his head.

The comm officer performed a survey. "Sir. The attack was done by the Galactic Federation."

"What?" Dallas was more infuriated. "I didn't think Harper would go this far."

"He made a deal with the devil." Arliss clenched his fists. "What's left of his soul is completely dark. Are there any signs of life?"

"Negative." The comm officer shook his head. "No human or animal survived this massacre."

"This will cause a rift between the Galactic Federation, for sure." Dallas shook his head.

"Revelation prophesied that there would be a great war that occurs in the first part of the Tribulation. I guess this starts it." Arliss was convinced. "We need to get to the base quickly. They may make another pass just to make sure. We don't want to be here for that."

The comm officer spoke up. "Wait! I have got a faint signal. Coming close to San Antonio."

"A life force?"

"One or two. One is definitely human."

"Send a rescue squad," Dallas commanded. "Make it quick, though. I'm giving the squad one hour."

February 25, 433 AE 09:02 FT, Near San Antonio, Texas

Elizabeth Potter woke up with a start. She felt a great deal of pain in her arms and chest. She stood up and looked all around her. The entire farm was black. The house was gone, as were all the barns. She saw a burning corpse sitting on what remained of the front deck. Her mother.

Elizabeth tried to make her way over, but she stumbled and fell. Then she heard a faint whimpering. She looked to her left and saw a young dog lying down inside a barrel.

"Max." She managed to crawl over to him, and she petted the poor dog on his head. She looked over at the pasture and saw several burned carcasses that used to be her father's cattle. She remembered seeing the ships come down and wondered why the Galactic Federation would do this. The sadness turned to anger as she turned to see one of the oval-shaped battle crafts land. Her eyes widened in terror, and she crawled into the barrel with Max.

A man in a soldier's uniform appeared before her, and she leaped out and began to hit him with fists. But another soldier grabbed her from behind. She screamed loudly.

"Calm down, miss." A woman in a medical suit appeared. "My name is Andrea. We are not the ones who did this."

"How can I be sure?" Elizabeth calmed down slightly.

"If we were the ones who did this, you would already be dead."

Elizabeth realized that made a lot of sense. Did the Asiatic-Russian Alliance get a hold of Federation battle crafts?

"No. All will be explained. Right now, you need medical attention. We need to get you back to the battleship."

Elizabeth nodded and the man who was holding her, picked her up and placed her on a hover stretcher that had been brought out. They made their way up the ramp and into the battlecraft.

February 26, 433 AE 07:34 FT, Battleship

Elizabeth woke up again in a medical room. She had blacked out during the trip up to the battleship. She tried to sit up but could barely move. She looked up to see a middle-aged woman in a doctor's uniform standing nearby.

"Elizabeth, my name is Aphra. I'm the chief medical officer on this ship."

"You are not military." Elizabeth noted. "I am from a military family; I can tell. Even the medical staff are different."

"You are correct. We are opposing the prime minister's plan."

"Rebels. The prime minister won't be pleased."

"The prime minister ordered the attack on the planet."

"What? Impossible. Why would he do such a thing?"

"In response to the other resistance force who took control of Washington, the force run by General Potter."

Elizabeth shook her head. "No. There is no way that my father would do that. Sure, he disagreed with some of the prime minister's ideas. But he disagreed with some of the former prime minister's ideas, too. He didn't take control of Washington then."

"I'm sorry to tell you that. But it's all over the news." Aphra told her.

"What's the difference between this rebel force and the other one?"

"The other force does not believe in Jehovah. We do. The other force is willing to start a war. Our only goal is to survive and provide shelter for anyone who seeks it."

Elizabeth scoffed. "Jehovah—you mean the deity that cult follows. Are you insane?"

"That deity is someone I opposed most of my life. My people followed a false deity called Allah, but we were wrong. Now that I believe, I know that all my sins are forgiven. Jehovah is a forgiving God and sent his Son to die on the cross for our sins."

"I've heard about that, but it seems ridiculous to me. I believe in what I can see."

"What do you believe happens when we die?"

"We cease to exist."

"If you are wrong, wouldn't you like to know beforehand?" Aphra sat in the chair next to her.

Elizabeth paused for a moment. "I guess so."

"It says in Romans 3:23 'For all have sinned and fall short of the glory of God.'"

"Well, that is morbid. I thought you said he was a forgiving God."

"I did. Romans 6:23 says 'For the wages of sin is death, but the gift of God is eternal life through Christ Jesus our Lord.'"

"So, he really died on the cross for our sins? When did this take place? Where? Why is it not written in history books?"

"Because scholars to this day oppose putting things that cannot be physically proven in textbooks, even though there are gaps in the theory of evolution that still can't be explained. These events happened between 0 BC and 0 AD. BC stands for 'Before Christ' and AD 'After Death.'"

"I don't remember those time periods."

"They occurred before most humans left Earth."

"Wait a minute. You're from Earth?"

"Yes. Somehow most who believed in Jehovah and Allah and another religious group were left behind when humans thought the Earth's star was going to collapse, but it did not. We existed for four hundred years, waiting for humans to return. Do you see how significant this is?"

"I'm starting to. So, what is considered wrong in Jehovah's eyes?"

"Having affairs outside of marriage."

Elizabeth frowned. "I had an affair with my husband's brother. Now they both are dead."

"Hey, that's okay. Jehovah loves all of us. No matter what we have done. Stealing, murder, lying, serving a false God. See? I am not perfect. It took all the vanishings to wake me up."

"The vanishings, was that foretold?"

"Yes. Some call that the Rapture, where God takes those who already believe to Heaven before the seven-year tribulation. Did you get the barcode marked on your body?"

"No. My father would not allow them to do so in Texas."

"That's good because those who accept the mark will never enter Heaven."

"So, his Son suffered and died for all of our sins—no matter how large?"

"No matter how large. Do you believe what he did for you now?"

Elizabeth paused again. Somehow, she knew that what she was listening to was true. Her mother had joined the cult and was allowed to visit her once a year. She had always seen a peace in her mother's eyes but could never explain it. This made perfect sense.

"Yes. I do believe. How can I accept this forgiveness?"

"Are you willing to live a life according to Christ's will for you?"

"Yes. I am willing."

"Then close your eyes and repeat after me."

Elizabeth closed her eyes, and Aphra stood and placed a hand on her forehead. Aphra turned to see that Arliss stood in the doorway. He nodded and remained silent.

"Jehovah, my Father in Heaven," Aphra began.

"Jehovah, my Father in Heaven,"

"I understand that I am a sinner."

"I understand that I am a sinner." Elizabeth repeated.

"I believe that you sent your Son to die on the cross for my sins," Aphra continued.

"I believe that you sent your Son to die on the cross for my sins."

"I promise to live a life according to your will."

"I promise to live a life according to your will." Elizabeth felt a peace filling her body and mind. She began to cry out of a deep joy.

"Come into my heart and wash my sins away." Aphra smiled.

"Come into my heart and wash my sins away." Elizabeth gave a quick but peaceful laugh among her tears.

"In your Son's Holy name, I pray."

"In your Son's Holy name, I pray."

"Amen."

"Amen," Elizabeth finished and produced a big smile.

Arliss stepped into the room. "Welcome, my new sister in Christ. How are you feeling?"

"Very well. Thank you, um . . ."

"Arliss Mars. Chief of security."

Aphra began her report. "She was lucky enough to escape without any major injuries. She had lost a lot of blood, but I gave her a transfusion, and she appears to be recovering nicely."

"Good. We'll have a room set up for her as soon as she is released."

"I was wondering if she would like to be my roommate." Aphra turned toward Elizabeth with a pleading look.

"That would be wonderful." Elizabeth smiled. "How soon can I be released?"

"I will go complete the paperwork now." Aphra quickly left the room.

CHAPTER SEVENTEEN
Tarsus, AD 35

Members of the Sanhedrin, religious authority of this day, stood in the temple and watched as a group of synagogue members dragged a young man into the temple and threw him on the floor at their feet.

"What is the meaning of this?" One of the Sanhedrin spoke up.

One of his captors replied, "This man is called Stephen. We have witnesses who testify that he has spoken words of blasphemy against Moses and against God. He claims that Jesus of Nazareth will destroy this place and change the customs Moses handed down to us."

The three witnesses came forward and testified for about ten minutes as the Sanhedrin listened intently.

The High Priest stepped out from among his Sanhedrin brothers and spoke to Stephen. "Is what they are saying true?"

Stephen stood up and looked at his accusers and then at the high priest. "Brothers and fathers, listen to me! The God of glory appeared to our father Abraham while he was still in Mesopotamia, before he lived in Haran. Leave your country and your people, God said, and go to the land I will show you.

"So, he left the land of the Chaldeans and settled in Haran. After the death of his father, God sent him to the land where you are now living. He gave him no inheritance here, not even a foot of ground. But God promised him that he and his descendants after him would possess the land, even though at that time Abraham had no children. God spoke to him in this way. 'Your descendants will be strangers in a country not their own, and they will be enslaved and treated four hundred years. But I will punish the nation they serve as slaves, and afterward they will come out of that country and worship me in this place."

Stephen continued for a while, and then the crowd became enraged and started to yell slanderous things, baring their teeth angrily at him. Then he looked up and smiled as he spoke again.

"Look, I see heaven open and the Son of Man standing at the right hand of God."

The crowd rushed him and dragged him out to the street. Someone threw a stone, which hit him squarely in the back. He began to pray.

"Lord Jesus, receive my spirit."

Another stone hit him on the side of his head and as blood dripped from his right ear, he got onto his knees and continued to pray.

"Lord, do not hold this sin against them."

Then two stones simultaneously hit him. On the left forearm and one in the back of his head. He fell to the ground in a puddle of blood and breathed his last breath. One particular man stood among the crowd. Saul silently approved of the death. To him, all disciples should be persecuted and put to the sword for the blasphemous words they speak.

February 26, 433 AE 19:25 FT, Battleship

Arliss stood by his office window and watched as Texas disappeared from sight. The ship could not use high-powered speed because of the trail they would leave. So, what normally would take one hour would take a little over a day. He looked at his desk at the picture of his wife and children. He specifically focused on the image of his son, Travis. He felt easier with the knowledge that his son was in a better place with Jehovah. He still missed him deeply and could not wait until they would be reunited in the Millennial Kingdom.

He glanced at the digital clock above the door, which read 05:19:25:37. Surprised at how much time had gone by in what felt like minutes, he made his way to the door.

"Lights off."

The room faded to dark as the door slid open, and he walked out into the dim hallway. He made his way down the hall and to an elevator. The elevator took him to the floor below, and he ran into Dallas on his way out.

"Worked a bit late, huh?" Dallas stated.

"Lost track of time." Arliss smiled. "Good thing we're not paid by the hour. Someone in HR would be furious."

They both laughed.

"I remember those days. My assistant constantly reminded me to leave before it came to that. She was such a good assistant. Vanished with the others. I did not even know she believed in Jehovah. Most are outspoken about their faith and wear it with a sense of pride. But she was more restrictive about who she told. I did make it obvious about my dislike for the Children of Jehovah, so I do not blame her. I used to be a scary individual if you were on the wrong end of a disagreement. What about you?" Dallas was curious.

"Not really supportive or opposed to them," Arliss replied. "Tried to keep emotions out of it. It was a bit harder after I found out that my son wanted to join them. But I still didn't show irritation toward them."

"You saw him vanish, right?"

Arliss answered. "Yes. On the trip to Earth. We were talking in the living room."

The elevator door slid open again, and Arliss and Dallas moved out of the way as a couple of security officers made their way out of the elevator and walked down the hall.

"Must have been more traumatic for you having a child disappear as opposed to an assistant."

"I had a heart attack."

"Oh, dear."

"Yep. My wife came in and found me. For all she knew he had left a pile of clothes on the couch as usual."

They laughed.

Arliss continued, "I vaguely remember her trying to contact him as she followed my hover stretcher to the medical bay. Probably numerous times."

"Yeah. Well, I've got to get some shut-eye."

"Same here. See you tomorrow."

"You bet."

Dallas walked down the hall one way, and Arliss made his way down the other. After a couple of turns, he walked through a sliding door and into his apartment. Marion and Paula sat on the table with a just-prepared dinner. Mashed potatoes, green beans, cornbread, some juicy steaks, and some mushroom gravy to pour over everything. A bottle of his favorite ale sat in front of his normal seat at the end of the table.

"Oh, my." Arliss enjoyed the nice smell of cooked meat. "What's the occasion?"

"Don't tell me you forgot your own birthday?" Marion shook her head.

Arliss sighed as his memory returned. "Silly me. Of course. Well, this is nice. Is that actual steak rather than the synthetic ones?"

"You bet. Dallas found a cow that was meant for slaughtering on the planet. He dropped it off not too long ago."

"Wow. Yeah, I ran into him on the way here. Come to think of it, that was a bit odd, him coming from this direction. I'll have to thank him tomorrow." Arliss sat down. "Allow me to lead us in prayer."

Everyone held hands, closed their eyes, and bowed their heads.

"Heavenly Father, thank you so much for this wonderful meal. Thank you for good friends like Dallas, my lovely wife, Marion, who is an excellent cook, and my two beautiful girls. In Your holy . . ."

A small blast was heard, and Arliss quickly stood up and to the side while he drew his blast revolver. He saw a figure in black clothing struggling. The man's blast revolver had backfired, and his shoulder was bloody. He tried to aim his weapon at Arliss again, but as he moved his arm up, a blast came from Arliss' gun and hit the intruder right in the chest. The would-be assassin dropped his blast gun and fell on his back.

As the attacker lay motionless on the floor, Arliss turned on his comm badge. "Security, this is Chief Security Officer Arliss Mars. A man just tried to kill me in my quarters."

"Copy that." A voice came through. "A team is enroute now."

"Thank you. I believe he is dead now."

"Understood."

Arliss turned to see his wife and Paula come out from under the table. Just then a bell rang at the door.

"Come in," Arliss responded.

The door slid open, and four guards rushed in, while two more officers remained outside.

One guard knelt and checked the intruder's pulse. "He's dead. Did he get a shot off?"

Arliss explained. "Sort of. He tried to shoot me in the middle of a prayer. His weapon backfired. That's the wound on his arm and shoulder."

"Well, that was lucky. We'll take him to the medical bay and then have him identified and torched."

"Good."

Two of the officers picked up the body and dragged it out. Then the third guard sprayed a cleansing chemical that dissolved the blood, and the fourth guard checked the other rooms for intruders. The fourth guard came out of the last bedroom.

"All clear. Commander Dallas is on his way. We're leaving the other two guards right outside just in case."

"Okay."

After all the guards left, Arliss turned to his family. "We all know that luck had nothing to do with that. Dinner's still good I think."

He sat down and picked up his fork and then noticed all of them looking at him with puzzled looks on their faces.

"Oh, yeah." He closed his eyes and lowered his head. "In Your holy name. Amen."

"How can you eat after that?" Marion was stunned.

"Simple. I am not going to let a good meal with my family be wasted by some would-be assassin. Don't worry; God's protecting us."

Paula smiled. "He sure is. Anyone else want to try?"

She looked around. "Nope. Okay. Let's dig in."

February 27, 433 AE 12:25 FT, Battleship

Arliss woke up to see 06:12:25:07 on the clock above his bedroom door. He jumped out of bed and raced to put his suit and holstered gun on. He dashed into the main room where Paula stood in the middle of the room with a silver mug of coffee ready to go.

"Thanks." He grabbed it. "Where's everyone else?"

Paula answered. "Marion is at her job. She killed your alarm, so you could get more sleep."

"Okay. That will do for now. Thanks for the coffee. See you later."

"You bet."

The front door slid open, and Arliss walked out. The four guards outside began to follow him, and he stopped.

"No. Two of you stay there, and two of you follow me."

"Our orders state . . ."

"If Dallas has a problem, tell him to talk to me."

"Very well, sir."

Two of the guards returned to their positions on either side of the door and the remaining two followed him down the hall and onto the elevator.

He made his way over to his office, and the guards entered before him and, when all was clear, left to their posts right outside.

He went past the guards into his office, sat down, and sipped his coffee. Then he started going over the security videos for the areas in and around his apartment. He had requested a copy of them before he turned in for the night. Not that he did not trust the officers, but he was adamant about knowing how the would-be killer got into his quarters. He would not let that happen again.

At Same Time in the Mess Hall

Paula sat across from a guy named Richard with a sad look on her face.

"Worried about your foster father?" Richard was concerned.

"Yeah." She ran a fork through her potato salad. "I can't believe someone would care enough to have him killed."

"Well, he is considered a traitor to the Federation. Plus, he was a particularly good soldier, so they see him as a big threat."

"You're not helping." Paula shook her head.

"Sorry. You know I'm here for you whenever you need me."

"Yes. I know." She finally took a bite of her food.

She decided that she would go to the Bible study for women that she had been invited to. She had questions about dating during the tribulation.

"What are your plans tonight?"

"I'm going to a Bible study in an hour. A friend invited me to that. But after that, I'm free."

"Good. I am going to one as well. It is held in Pastor Chekov's quarters. We are going over the qualifications of elders. What about yours?"

"This is my first time, so I'm not sure."

"Okay. Well, I was hoping I could invite you to attend a concert in the conference hall. A symphony will be performing hits from Earth composers like um . . . Beethoven, I think was one name."

"Sure. That sounds like fun." Paula smiled and took another bite of her lunch. "How was your evening?"

"Well, it was less eventful than yours. I played some basketball with a few friends. Administrative staff versus security officers. We actually won!"

"Wow, that's good."

"By negative seventeen points."

They both laughed.

CHAPTER EIGHTEEN

March 12, 433 AE 14:45 FT, Oxford Military Station in Orbit around the Planet Britain

A tall commander stood on the bridge of the space station and noted the high military presence. Fifteen battleships stood at the ready on orders of the prime minister, seven more than normal. Tensions were high everywhere. Two-fifths of the fleet broke ranks and joined what has been called the Texas Rebellion. He could not believe the audacity of the prime minister to call this rebellion small in the grand scheme of things. In fact, the attack on Texas was the worst way to go. But the commander held true to the belief that the Federation would be the right side to stand with.

Just as that thought entered his head, a small fleet of five battleships appeared. Then forty more behind them.

The comm officer spoke up. "Sir, a signal is coming through."

"Put them on." The commander was afraid that this could be the rebellion.

His fears were confirmed when General Potter appeared on the screen.

"Commander. Do you stand with us or the Federation?"

"I stand with the Federation, of course. Certainly, you can be . . ."

The screen went blank, and the incoming battleships began firing. The ship shook wildly as it took heavy fire.

The engineering officer spoke in a panicked voice. "Sir. We are losing shields fast."

The ship continued to shake.

"Send out the surrender beacon."

"Surrender beacon sent, sir." The engineering officer paused. "They destroyed it."

At the Same Time outside the Station

Outside, the incoming ships destroyed each of the battleships in a quick fashion. All the wreckage was pulled into the atmosphere and burned. The station began to break apart. Then the incoming ships halted as a large explosion occurred, leaving tons of debris, which quickly fell into the atmosphere. Most burned up, but a large part of the station made its way through and landed in the middle of the city of London.

People ran everywhere as one ship entered the atmosphere. On large screens all over the city, General Potter appeared. People stopped and looked at the screens.

"This is General Potter of the Rebellion. You all have a decision to make. Join me in the war against the evil tyrant, Alex Harper, who wiped out an entire planet, or do not join. I will not attack those who do not join me, but I will imprison them in concentration camps. If you are with me, raise your hands."

All the survivors raised their hands to signify their support.

March 12, 433 AE 15:05 FT, London Manufacturing Plant

A small landing craft arrived at the front gates, and General Potter exited the craft, followed by twenty soldiers in battle gear. He walked up to the front as the two guards came out of their booth.

"We cannot open this gate without Federation approval." The first guard spoke up.

"Is that so, son?" Potter looked back at his armed soldiers. "What do you think your chances are?"

The second guard turned and pulled the lever on the side. The doors started to open.

"What are you doing?" The first guard drew his weapon and aimed it at the guard.

The twenty soldiers spread out and aimed their guns at him.

"I would drop that blast rifle, son."

He dropped his weapon, and two soldiers rushed over and put him in handcuffs.

"Take him to the concentration camp," Potter added before turning to the second soldier.

"What's your name, son?"

"Lieutenant Aaron Ransom, from Texas."

Potter understood why Ransom had sided with him. "How many of the new battleships have been completed?"

Ransom spoke up. "Thirty. And ten more are almost complete."

"Have you been on a battleship before?"

"Yes, sir. But they demoted me after the Texas attack."

"Their mistake. What was your rank before?"

"Commander of that fleet you just destroyed."

"I guess their demotion saved you then. How would you like to command one of those new battleships?"

A wide grin appeared on Ransom's face. "It would be an honor, sir. And if I had been in command, everyone would have been saved because I would have surrendered the planet immediately."

March 17, 433 AE 13:15 FT, In Orbit of Arctican

A single battleship appeared on the screen. On the bridge stood Commander Dallas, Arliss Mars, and the rest of the ship's chief officers. Arliss and Dallas remained silent for a moment as they stared at the planet.

"It's not much to look at, but this is the main base of operations. The base is hidden inside one of the mountains. The launching pad is three miles north. We land there, and then we have to make our way through to the actual base."

"Not all at once, right?" Arliss cautioned.

"That's right. One group of twenty each. We only take down the first four groups. Temporary tents will house the groups that are on deck. Once the last group leaves, we will send four more groups. The process will take a while. Leaders will go first, most of them. I will be on the last group."

"Me, too," Arliss agreed.

Dallas shook his head. "Andrew wants you in the first group along with nine other security guards. Then two engineers, including our chief engineer, our lead doctor, and a team of nurses. He needs the leaders set up—security and medical staff especially. A member of the staff is suffering from hypothermia, and we have no real doctors yet."

"I'll inform our doctor." Arliss took one last look at the planet and then headed off the bridge.

March 18, 433 AE 12:25 FT, In Orbit of Arctican

Aphra was at the front doors of the medical bay, going over the supplies that were being loaded for the first ship down. The doors slid open, and Arliss walked in.

"Just the man I needed to see." Aphra swiped the screen on her pad a few times. "I have a list of nurses to send down in the first four groups."

Arliss took the pad and looked at the list. "Very good. One change, though. They want you in the first group."

"I'm staying until the last group."

"Orders are orders. They want both of us there. They have no real doctor and some sick people who need a real doctor."

Aphra reluctantly agreed. "Okay then. Bump the last name on the list and put me in that place."

"You got it. We leave in one hour. Are all the supplies packed?"

"Should be. I'm just going over them one last time, and then I'll have the staff bring the crates over."

"Good." He handed the pad back to her. "I'll see you there."

After Arliss left, Aphra shut the crate and made her way back to her assistant's office. She notified her assistant about the change in plans and then left the medical bay to go pack her belongings.

She made it through the busy sections with relative ease and went up the elevator to her floor. She rushed to her apartment where Elizabeth sat, reading a pad.

"Change of plans, roomy," she explained as Elizabeth looked up. "I have to go on the first group, too."

"Wow. Do you need help packing?"

"Not really. All I have is in this small bag." She reached under her bed and pulled out a backpack. She opened the backpack and confirmed that all her things were packed. Then Aphra zipped the backpack shut and slung it over her back.

Elizabeth stood, and they hugged. "I'm on the last group, so it might be a day or two before we see each other again."

"Well, until then." They hugged once more and then Aphra rushed out of the room and out of sight. Elizabeth sat down and picked her pad up to continue reading.

May 17, 433 AE 14:00 FT, Planet Earth, Jerusalem

Alex Harper stood in his office on the highest floor of the tallest tower in the new Jerusalem. The city had been built quickly and was more majestic than any other city. He glanced toward the center to see his statue standing almost as high, and he beamed with delight. It was General Wu's idea to build a statue in his honor, but he truly admired the idea. It was made of solid bronze and stood out among everything else in the city as the sun shone off it.

He then looked down at all the people scurrying about, preparing for a week-long festival in his honor—a festival that would have lots of food, dancing, wine, and much more.

Then the front door to his office slid open, and one of his assistants walked in with a nervous look on his face.

"What now?" He hoped it was not anything that would ruin his mood.

"Sir. Potter's fleet has captured the planet Britain and one of the manufacturing plants of the new battleships."

Alex walked over to his desk and opened the first drawer. He pulled out a blast pistol, aiming the gun at the assistant, who quickly got to his knees.

"Please, sir. I'm just the messenger."

"The messenger, yes of course. Did you know that in times of war, most kings would cut off the head of messengers and send them back to their leader? For heaven's sake, stand up, you buffoon."

The assistant stood up as he began to sweat.

Alex walked over to him and jammed the gun into the side of his head. "I could blast you all over this room. Leave tons of evidence. Hell, I could even walk out and tell everyone that I shot you. You know what they would do? Nothing. Absolutely nothing. Because they worship me. I am their god. They fear me, they love me, and they worship me."

The assistant began to cry.

Then Alex began to laugh, and he pulled the gun away and tossed it on his desk. "Now go tell the general that I want him here immediately!"

"Yes, sir." The assistant ran out of the room as a bunch of staff members peered in. He looked over at them, and they all quickly went about their business as the doors shut. Suddenly, the building began to shake violently, and Alex fell onto the floor.

At the Same Time, Outside the Building

Outside, the whole city began to shake violently. Not just in the city but all over the planet. All over the galaxy, all the planets began to shake. Violently, buildings began to topple, and monuments fell. The statue of the prime minister toppled over and broke in half. The bottom half landed on a few buildings and the top half fell into the man-made river that surrounded Jerusalem's center.

May 17, 433 AE 13:53 FT, Arctican

Arliss followed the group leader up the icy ledge, and the rest of the group followed him. The cold wind swept past his face and blew snow at him hard. He could barely see a few feet ahead of him.

"Should we stop and rest?" he asked the guide.

"Negative. The storm will last for hours. If we stop, we will die. We are only a half a mile from the closest entrance. It should be about twenty more minutes at the most."

"Okay." Arliss continued to follow the leader up the icy path that was only about ten feet wide until it dropped into a large valley.

A few more minutes passed, and suddenly the ground began to shake violently.

"Earthquake!" the guide shouted. "Hurry. We are almost there! But the guide slipped and fell over the edge and was gone. Then Aphra tumbled over and started slide toward the edge. Just as she fell over, Arliss managed to leap over and grab her. But the shaking continued, and he fell over with her. He managed to stab his stake, and they slid down a way and hung there as the mountain finally stopped shaking.

Then the whole ledge above them started to give way.

"Oh, Lord, help us!" Arliss cried out.

"Over there." Aphra pointed past him over to a large hole a little below them.

Arliss hung a rope to the stake with one hand. He pulled Aphra up onto his back and swung around. He managed to land his feet just inside the hole. Aphra climbed her way inside, and then Arliss slipped and almost fell over, but Aphra grabbed him and pulled him in just before tons of ice fell past them.

"God is watching out for us." Aphra smiled.

"He truly is." Arliss stuck his head out to look up, and he quickly pulled himself back inside as more ice fell past them. "That was one heck of an earthquake."

"Look!" She pointed further into the hole where a metal wall stood. "That could be the inside of the base."

Two Hours Later

After a couple hours of pounding, Arliss and Aphra sat on the ground and shivered. The climbing stake had fallen so climbing back up was not an option.

"Funny," Aphra laughed, "they wanted me on the first group to treat someone with hypothermia. Now we might fall to that as well."

"D-don't worry. J-J-Jehovah didn't s-save us just to l-let us d-d-die," Arliss assured her. He could not feel any of his limbs, and he started to pass out until something whacked him on the side of his head.

He looked over to see Aphra with a raised hand. "Don't you quit on me, Mars! Stay awake."

She sat back down and looked away, and then a light appeared in front of them. In the light stood a figure of a man.

"Have no fear, my children. Help is near."

The light disappeared, and then a drill shot through the wall leaving a large hole. A man stepped through and pulled Aphra to her feet. He handed her out to other rescue workers and then pulled Arliss to his feet.

"Let's get them to the medical bay, ASAP!" he shouted. "We need to warm them up."

May 18, 433 AE 10:52 FT, Arctican

Arliss woke up and found himself in a bath of warm water. He looked over next to him and saw a middle-aged man in a black jacket with dashing blonde hair.

"Arliss Mars." The man stepped forward. "I'm Andrew Larkendome."

"Nice to meet you, sir."

"Please, call me Andrew. It seems that God really wants you to live."

"What about the others?"

"They made it inside in time. Lost one of them and the guide. But everyone else is doing fine."

"Good. Looks like you'll have to find a new entrance."

"We have a couple others. A bit longer of a trek, but the other groups are on their way. The earth did not just shake here. All the planets shook. The prime minister's statue was among the casualties."

"I'll bet he's upset."

"He didn't show it in the press conference. But I would not take that bet."

Arliss stood up and grabbed a towel. "He does have a temper, especially now that he's the Antichrist. Before Aphra and I were rescued, I saw a black figure in a bright light. He said to have no fear and called us his children."

"Aphra mentioned that." Andrew nodded. "It seems you have an important role to play. I am not sure what, but I'm sure that Jehovah will reveal his plans in time."

CHAPTER NINETEEN
May 21, 433 AE 21:15 FT, Arctican

Aphra sat in her new quarters, which were not even half the size of her old quarters. She shared a bunk room with four other women. One would be Elizabeth as soon as she arrived. In the bunk above her was Ariola Mills. Ariola was one of the nurses that came on the first expedition. Her brother, James, was the nurse who was killed in the earthquake. Across from Aphra sat Cassandra Reed. Cassandra was a security guard and had a muscular build with blonde hair that was normally tied up in a ponytail, but this night, her hair was messy and free. She also snored very loudly.

"Gosh!" Ariola woke up. "Please let me put a sock in her mouth."

"I'm sure we'll get used to it after time." Aphra crawled into her bed and pulled the covers over her.

"Are you ready for the next day on this dump?"

"Hey. We need to have a good attitude about this. The important thing is that the Lord has kept us safe and has helped us find a base that will be hard to find."

"He didn't keep my brother safe." Ariola started to cry. "I don't know how I can go on."

"Just remember that he is waiting for us in the Millennial Kingdom and that he is safe and in a place of eternal peace."

"I'll try. Thank you, Doctor."

"Aphra, please."

"Thank you, Aphra."

"You're welcome, and sorry in advance."

"Huh?"

"I snore, too." Aphra pulled the covers over her head.

"Oh, bother."

Aphra quickly fell asleep but woke up to find herself in a desert similar to one close to her home. The sun shone brightly in her eyes, and she shielded them with her arms. After getting used to the daylight, she removed her arms and looked around. Off in the distance, she saw a city that looked like the New Jerusalem. The city was burning to the ground and was quickly hidden by a large cloud of black smoke.

Aphra turned to see a figure walking closer to her.

As the black figure got close the blackness faded and the figure was revealed to be Katrina Nova.

"Katrina!" Aphra ran over and hugged her. "I thought I . . ." Aphra paused. "I'm dreaming."

"It's okay, Aphra. I am at peace now, and I have been sent to deliver a message."

"What message?"

"There are battles to come: monsters from the earth, disease, and famine, but Jehovah will watch over his children. Those who accept him into their hearts will be protected. I will return for the final battle as will other martyrs."

Suddenly large black wings appeared behind Katrina. She turned and flew up high into the sky.

Aphra woke up with a start. She sat up and bumped her head against the top bunk.

"Ow!"

She held her head and looked up to see Arliss, Cassandra, Ariola, and Andrew standing by her bed.

"You okay there?" Arliss asked.

"I'll get some ice." Ariola made her way out of the room.

"What's wrong?"

"You've been asleep for a week."

After getting something to eat in the mess hall and icing her head. Aphra told Arliss and Andrew about the vision she had.

"The Bible does say that the martyrs will have a special place in heaven," Andrew told her. "This is a confirmation of what I already know. The Bible says that scorpion-like creatures will come out of the earth and attach to those who do not have the Lord's protection. It also says that there will be a plague and famine that spreads throughout the land. The earthquake happened on all the planets simultaneously. There will be an even greater one in the second half of the tribulation."

"What about the two witnesses?" Arliss was curious. "I can't believe they didn't come with us."

"They are still preaching. The temple is about the only place in New Jerusalem that was left standing. I believe they have more protection than anyone else. Nothing has worked to kill them. Blast guns, knives, and swords—all sorts of weapons have failed," Andrew told them.

"Well, I need to get to work." Aphra stood up. "Has Elizabeth arrived yet?"

"Not yet. The last four groups are preparing to come down." Arliss explained. "She is worried about you, though. I should send word to them and let them know."

"Can I communicate with her?"

"Absolutely." Arliss nodded. "I'll arrange it."

May 28, 433 AE 20:54 FT, In Orbit around Arctican

Elizabeth jogged down the hall in her jogging clothes. She made her way back to her quarters and walked in. As the doors slid shut behind her, she sat down on the couch and started to take off her running boots when the telepad beeped.

"Answer." She looked up to see Aphra appear on the screen.

"Aphra," Elizabeth sighed. "Boy, am I glad to see you. I was so worried."

"Well, apparently time passes quicker when you have a vision from Jehovah."

"What?"

"I'll explain that later. You ready to come down?"

"You bet I am. All packed and ready to go. How's life there?"

"The quarters are cramped. We have two bunkmates, Cassandra and Ariola. Cassandra's a security guard, so we have extra protection."

"That's nice." Elizabeth smiled. "What about the food?"

"Military rations."

"Not too bad. My father had our family live on that stuff most of the time. You build up an immunity to the taste after time."

"I look forward to that."

"It takes ten years."

They both laughed.

Suddenly a voice appeared over the intercom system.

"Folks, this is Dallas speaking. A huge fleet has just surfaced and are demanding that we join them or get blown out of the sky. A fleet under command of the rebellion leader General Potter."

"I have to go. He won't destroy us if he knows I'm here."

"God be with you."

"You, too."

Elizabeth refastened her jogging boots and raced out of her quarters. She raced down the hall and took the elevator up. She got off and two soldiers stopped her before she entered the bridge.

"This is a restricted area, miss."

"The man that's about to blow us up is my father."

The guards quickly got out of the way.

Dallas pleaded. "General, we are not with the prime minister. But our ship is extremely low on crew. We could not be of good use to you."

"I don't care!" Potter shouted from the screen. "You are either with us or against us! I'll blow your ship to pieces."

"Don't you dare!" Elizabeth raced onto the bridge.

General Potter stood up out of his chair with a look of shock on his face.

"Lizzie."

"Yes, Father. It's me."

"Oh, thank heavens. I thought I lost you."

"I appear to be the only survivor. I was the only one smart enough to hide in the fields. I did get knocked unconscious, but I survived, and this crew found me. We have a community that harbors those who chose not to worship the prime minister as a god and worship Jehovah instead."

"You believe that nonsense?"

"It's not nonsense, father. Look at what is going on around us. The vanishings, the two witnesses. Even the earthquake on every single planet.

It is all evidence that Jehovah does exist, and he is watching out for us."

"The scientists have explained all that, not that it makes any sense."

"And who do those scientists work for?"

"The prime minister."

"He is the Antichrist. Who else would be bold enough to think of himself as a deity?"

"Let's talk about this over dinner." Potter sat down. "I want to be able to hold you."

"Yes."

"I'll send a vessel over to pick you up."

"I'll be waiting."

May 28, 433 AE 21:11 FT, Arctican

Aphra stood with Andrew on top of the base's roof, which was basically ground covered in snow, and she looked up into space. She could barely make out the battleship that had carried them to the base. But the ship was not their real protector. Jehovah was the only one who could claim that.

Andrew broke the silence, "There are trying times ahead, but Jehovah will protect us."

"I know." Aphra looked down into the valley. "I am so blessed to have found him when I did. I was hoping my husband would not divorce me, but he did. His heart was hardened long ago when our daughter died from sickness. Were you married?"

"My wife died of an incurable cancer years before this. Even with all the advances in medicine, there are still some diseases that cannot be cured without a miracle."

"Leukemia?" She asked.

"That's curable," Andrew told her.

"Too bad Earth wasn't rediscovered four years ago." Aphra looked down.

"Yeah. How old was your daughter?"

"Two. Do you believe she is in heaven?"

"Yes. I believe at a certain age when they are still too young to understand things like God, they will be instantly saved if they die at that point."

"I have to believe that." She looked up again.

Suddenly Aphra felt her pulling close to Andrew. She wondered if this was right. It felt real and good as she let him bend forward and plant a kiss on her lips. But just as they kissed, they heard a loud explosion, and they both looked up to see fire in the sky where the battleship once was.

"No!" Aphra screamed, and Andrew held onto her as she almost fell over. "Elizabeth."

The door to the base stairwell lifted, and Arliss ran up onto the roof and looked at the sky in horror as pieces of the ship fell into orbit and burned up in the atmosphere.

"Marion!"